Kenzie's story

{MELODY CARLSON}

{ryun's story}

{ryun's story}

WIGGINS HIGH SCHOOL LIBRARY

degrees of betrayal

JEFF NESBIT

Tyndale House Publishers, Inc.
Wheaton, Illinois

Library of Congress Cataloging-in-Publication Data

Nesbit, Jeffrey Asher.
  Ryun's story / Jeff Nesbit.
    p. cm. — (Degrees of betrayal)
  Summary: Ryun is a self-centered soccer star, living it up his senior year in high
school by cheating on his girlfriend with her best friend, smoking, drinking, stealing,
and lying, until a serious car accident and its aftermath change everything.
  ISBN 1-4143-0003-4 (sc)
  [1. Soccer—Fiction. 2. Korean Americans—Fiction. 3. Conduct of life—Fiction.
4. Traffic accidents—Fiction. 5. Interpersonal relations—Fiction.] I. Title. II. Series.
  PZ7.N4378Ry 2004
  [Fic]—dc22   2004001501

Printed in the United States of America

08 07 06 05 04
 7   6   5   4   3   2   1

To Casey, Josh, Elizabeth, and Daniel
Life is a journey.
I'm so proud of all of you
for finding your own path.

I know she doesn't like this sort of thing,
but here it is anyway:

Thanks, Ramona, for all the work
you put into this.

I am invincible.

You don't believe me? Really? Well, watch this.

There used to be a straight road, about a quarter of a mile long, out near the airport. It was behind a couple of big warehouses. If the word got around, and you heard about it, you could watch two kids racing their cars just as it was getting dark.

They'd hit 120 mph or so, hope they didn't slide or fishtail at the end, and then get out of there before the cops could catch them. Every so often, a kid would roll, get mangled, and die or something.

Then the cops started hanging around, waiting. The city put up speed bumps. Finally they cut the road in half.

But beneath that road is a huge empty water pipe. I don't know what it was used for. Maybe

carrying sludge from one of the factories to a stag-
nant pond at the other end.

But now the factory's gone, and the pond is only
dirt and trash. There's nothing at either end of this
long straight pipe. It simply sits there. Waiting
quietly, never complaining.

The pipe is just big enough for someone tall,
like me, to walk through. I'm 6'2", taller than
almost every other kid at Highview. I can walk
through that pipe and my straight black hair
doesn't even come close to touching the top. When
I spread my arms wide, they barely touch either
side. If you shout at one end, your voice disappears
at the other.

I don't ever walk through that pipe, though.
No, I leave an old Yamaha motorcycle out there,
and I ride whenever I feel like it. I don't wear a
helmet. I don't need to. I never wear a seat belt
in a car either . . . I told you—nothing touches me.
I always come out on top.

Anyway, the old Yamaha is one of those sport
bikes where you have to ride low, your head down.
I got it from one of my friends I play soccer with—
a lawyer—who was bored with it. I picked up a little
extra cash from my folks to pay for it.

They don't know I own it. My folks, I mean.
There's a lot they don't know, actually. There's a lot
everyone doesn't know . . . well, maybe except for
my little sister, Joon, but she'd never give me up.

Here's how it works. You start at one end of the
tunnel on the bike, get going, no lights. Then you
kick into another gear. The bike jolts forward a lit-

tle. You put your head down lower. The light starts to dim. It gets darker.

Then you hit a time—maybe just a few seconds, maybe forever—when it's pitch dark. There's only the sound of the bike coming off the walls of the tunnel to guide you. You hope the bike is going straight, but you don't really know. You aim at the tiny dot of light at the other end of the tunnel and hope you have it right. Maybe you do—maybe you don't.

But I always have it right. I always hit that spot of light at the other end of the tunnel. The bike doesn't wobble or pitch. I don't ever have to adjust. I just aim and ride through the darkness. And I hit it perfectly every time.

It's such a rush. Light to dark to light. Fast to faster. And then—you *rip* out the other end into the brilliant light, going at least 80 or 90 mph across the dirt toward a line of trees. Plenty of time to stop the bike.

I can do it 100 times, a million times. I never get tired of the feeling. There's a point where you can't be afraid, because you know that if you are, you'll lose it. The bike will roll or tilt, and it will all end. Your life, I mean. But when you know you're invincible, you're not afraid. You just go, as fast as you can, until you blast out the other end.

It's funny what happens when you live your life this way, as if you're untouchable. When I'm on a soccer field, there are times when I *know* I cannot be stopped. There may be one or two—or even three— defenders in my way. But I simply go around them, through them. I carry the ball with me as I go, and then I put the ball near post, upper 90, wherever it needs to be.

I've never told this to anyone. I'm not sure anyone would understand it or even believe it. I'm not sure anyone would even care. It isn't an easy thing to explain.

We all die some day. I know that. But not me right now, not this way. I am invincible. I can do what I want, when I want. It's just the way it is.

"Ryun!"

"What?" I asked, irritated.

"The game? Here? Today?"

"Um," I answered, glancing back at my coach blankly. *The game? What game? What's he talking about? All I can see is this amazing girl with the longest, shiniest auburn hair, falling delicately over both shoulders. She's sprawled sideways, every single possible curve of her body in profile just a few feet away from me. . . .*

"Do something!" my coach, Frank Jenkins, barked at the guy sitting next to me. My teammate responded by launching a soccer ball at my head. It bounced off, causing my head to whip back slightly. The ball rolled a few feet away from our team huddle.

"Hey!" I said, reluctantly pulling my gaze away from the girl with the deep, rich auburn hair. But not before she'd turned her head, catching my gaze for a moment. "You didn't need to . . ."

Coach Jenkins sighed. He wasn't the most patient man on the planet. He didn't know a whole lot about soccer, but he knew plenty about boys—and girls. "Are you with us now?"

I didn't blink or look away. It was something I'd learned a long time ago. It was the way you fooled your teachers, parents, or anybody else you felt like fooling. Just stare—as if you're giving that person your total undivided attention. Even if you aren't.

"Yeah, Coach, I'm with you." I nodded once firmly.

"And you heard what I was saying?"

Of course I hadn't heard what he was saying. It was 70 degrees, the first warm sunny day of spring, on a Saturday. A group of girls trying out new halter tops and brightly colored shorts had decided to come to our high school soccer match. They were sitting very close to our huddle at halftime. None of us had heard a word our coach was saying.

"Yeah, Coach, I heard," I lied. I glanced around the huddle. One of my teammates held up a hand and flashed a 4, 5, and then a 1 at me. I nodded slightly back at him, a small smile at the corners of my mouth. I'd have to thank him later.

"And are you okay with that?"

"Sure, Coach, no problem. I can handle it. You do what you gotta do."

We were getting killed in the middle. The team we were playing had two extraordinarily fast strikers, even by modest high school soccer standards. But worse yet, they had two big tough center mids, guys who were knocking our center mids off the ball over and over. Between those two central midfielders and the two strikers who kept running around our outside marking backs, we'd had a very long first half.

Surprisingly, though, the score was still 0-0. They'd hit a couple of posts with shots, and our goalkeeper had made a couple of really nice saves. But it was only a matter of time until they scored, unless our coach made a change.

Which he had. He was going to a 4-5-1 formation. That meant he was playing four defenders back and moving an extra midfielder into the middle of the park to help out against those two tough center mids. He was playing for a 0-0 tie, hoping he could hang on in the second half and not get run over by the team he was facing.

He was leaving me up top, all by myself. I was the "1" in that formation—the lone striker facing up to four defenders on their side at any given time. There was no way I should be able to score in this formation. No way. The coach was moving the defense back. If I was able to break through somehow and score, great. But mostly my job was to keep their defense honest.

I smiled. *Like there was anyone on this sorry field who could stop me.* High school soccer is bad. It isn't anything like my club team that played in tournaments all over the country against the best soccer players in my age-group in the United States.

About half the players on my high school soccer team hardly even knew what they were doing. They ran around and kicked the ball but didn't really know why. Opposing teams were much the same. Which meant I could do what I wanted against opposing teams in high school, almost at will, no matter how many defenders they threw at me.

"So you'll stay at midfield, look for long balls over the top?" my coach asked.

"Got it," I answered.

Coach Jenkins turned to our midfielders. "Look for Ryun long. You can send it to either flag, let him run on it. That'll stretch the field and . . ."

I stopped paying attention. I knew what he wanted. He didn't expect me to score, only scare their defense every so often. So we'd see. I knew that I'd take whatever they gave me.

I looked back at the group of girls nearby, singling out the cute girl I couldn't take my eyes off. Sierra Reynolds had been unreachable earlier in the year. She'd been dating a senior, Michael something-or-other. But he was graduating, and she had no choice now but to turn back to her own class, to juniors like me.

In fact, I was pretty sure she'd broken up with the guy after he'd taken early acceptance to college and lost interest in Sierra and everything else over the holidays. Which meant I had to move. Now.

I couldn't stop staring at her. I mean, it was mind-blowing. Some *really* interesting things had happened to her over the winter, when coats, sweaters, and long skirts hid every girl's shape. Nothing dramatic, but enough to grab my interest.

On a Saturday, in the warm spring sun, when there was no dress code and there were no teachers or parents around to say otherwise, I could see very clearly that Sierra had grown up a little over the past six months when no one was paying any attention. Or, at least, when *I* wasn't paying attention.

She was wearing cotton shorts and a bright yellow halter top. Now she was sitting with her head tilted back, her arms propped behind her back, her legs stretched out and crossed in front of her. *How had I not noticed her until now, until this very moment?*

Sierra glanced over. Even from where I was sitting, her big green eyes were riveting. I didn't look away. She didn't look away. We both smiled at the same time, as if on cue. I tapped my chest with one finger, pointed to the goal at the far end of the soccer field, held up one finger and then pointed back at Sierra. "For you," I mouthed.

Sierra nodded, laughing. She understood. I'd just promised to score a goal for her. No one else in the crowd, on the team, on the field, mattered. She looked away, then back to her group of friends.

As we meandered back onto the field to start the second half, I took one last look over at Sierra. She was doing her best to pretend she wasn't paying any attention to me. But I knew she was. And we'd see.

The first 30 minutes of the second half were brutal. The opposing team controlled 80 to 90 percent of the possession. They were pounding the ball at our defensive end, slotting balls through, taking them around and into our defense every conceivable way. But with nine defenders behind the ball, they were having a much more difficult time getting shots off.

I hardly even touched the ball. Every so often one of our defenders would kick the ball long, in a panic, and I'd chase it. But by the time I got to it, there were four or five from the other team chasing it too. I couldn't do much with it, not with those odds.

But with 10 minutes to go, the chance came. All of their midfielders were pressed forward, attacking. Two of their defenders had drifted over the midfield line, attacking also. It left me one on two with their remaining defenders.

The ball kicked out wide, almost by accident, and our outside right midfielder got to it first. I started my run perfectly, right as he launched it to the far flag. I timed it so that I was just onside as the ball was kicked. I glanced over at the assistant referee as I made my run. His flag was down. I was onside.

The ball rolled toward the far flag. I raced past first one and then the second defender. I caught up with the ball the instant it started to bounce more slowly. Settling the ball at my feet, I cut back sharply to goal, as I'd been taught by Asher James, my club coach, and every Olympic development coach I'd ever had.

And I did what every great striker does. Don't fool around. When you have the ball at your feet and a chance to score, take it to goal. Go right at it. Score.

The screams and shouts of the fans and my team-mates dimmed. The air rushed past me as I pushed the ball out in front—not too far to lose control, yet far enough to allow me to run at nearly top speed toward the goal. Their goalkeeper tried to time it, rush at me to force me into a bad last touch. Yeah, right. Like I was going to miss this one.

At the last possible moment, I flicked the ball with the outside of my left foot to the keeper's right, eluding his outstretched hands, and then cut the ball back to my right. I took three gigantic steps toward the empty net. Just before striking the ball, I glanced off to the side, in Sierra's direction, then buried the ball in the back of the net.

As my teammates rushed to the end of the field to mob me, I looked over to the side of the field again, finding Sierra. Her auburn hair glistened in the sun, and her green eyes flashed. I'd delivered, as promised. She knew it. I knew it. It was now her move.

3

Some people exist because they matter.
Others don't because they don't. It's as simple as
that, as far as I'm concerned.

As I walked off the field, there was a group of
girls gathered at the fence post, next to the gate
where we exited the stadium to head to the locker
room. Several of them flashed smiles at me. I flashed
a smile back. But I really had *one* girl in mind, and
I couldn't find her.

"Nice move to beat that goalkeeper, Ryun," someone said from another direction. I turned. I didn't
recognize the voice, but it was nice. It also wasn't
Sierra. It was some girl with mousy brown hair I'd
seen around the school. Some girl I had no interest
in. McKenzie, I think. But I wasn't sure.

She was nothing special. And I didn't like the girl

13

she was standing with—Anna Krenshaw, a quiet Chinese girl who'd been adopted and who carried her Christian faith around school like some badge of honor.

The Chinese girl I knew a little. The other girl? No clue, other than maybe her first name. She had no redeeming feature, nothing appealing. It took me all of two seconds to size her up, dismiss her, and move on. Next.

"Yeah, thanks," I said, not even bothering to make eye contact. I couldn't find Sierra. She'd vanished.

The girl with the mousy brown hair didn't give up though. "It was calm, that move with the outside of your left foot."

I turned back to the girl. "Huh? You saw that?"

The girl nodded. "Sure. The keeper thought you were going to your right. Taking it left like that took him completely . . ."

I'd spotted Sierra, so I didn't hear the other girl finish the sentence. But I didn't care. It was my job to score. It was what I did. It didn't mean I had to pay attention to my fans.

Sierra was walking away with a small group of girls, headed in a totally different direction from the locker room. I'd never meet up with her. I knew she was playing with me.

I glanced around the stadium. There were two exits back to the school on this side and a third exit on the far side of the stadium. I was moving toward one of the school-side exits. Sierra was headed out of the other with her friends. I had to move fast.

"Gotta go warm down," I said to no one in particular and took off in the opposite direction. I had to time it just right. I half-sprinted back across the field, toward the far exit.

As soon as I'd exited, I made a hard right and ducked behind the line of trees that flanked the stadium. I put it in high gear the length of the stadium to the far corner, made another hard right, and continued to sprint, the trees to my right.

I glanced once through the trees. Sierra and her friends were now at the exit. I took another right at the next corner and dropped down to a fast jog. I'd timed it exactly right. I got to the exit just as Sierra was leaving through the gate.

She looked left as I bore down on them. Our eyes locked. A very small smile crept across her face. She knew. It *was* her move. But I'd made it impossible for her to avoid.

I slowed even more as I approached them. The other girls all eyed Sierra, wondering.

Sierra took a step away from the group, toward me. "You won," she said in my direction.

"We did."

"Because of your goal."

"Always. They count on me."

Sierra glanced back at her friends, then back at me. "Why aren't you with your team now? Don't you have, like, a pep talk or something?"

I saw my opening. "Coach gave us the pep talk at halftime. I wasn't paying any attention."

"You weren't?"

"No, I was paying attention to you."

Sierra didn't even flinch. Not a bit. "I know," she said.

I tilted my head in her direction. "You know that goal . . . ?"

". . . was for me?"

"Yeah, it belongs to you. It goes in your scrapbook."

Sierra laughed. "But I don't like soccer. I don't understand it."

"You don't need to. My teammates give the ball to me, and I score."

"That's it?"

"Simple as that."

We eyed each other. There were no others. Sierra's friends nearby, my teammates off in the distance—they didn't matter. There was only us. The next move. The next words.

Sierra reached in her purse. She pulled a digital camera out of it, held it up, and snapped a picture of me. It happened so fast, before I could react.

"There!" she said, smiling.

"What's that for?"

"The yearbook. It'll make a nice picture."

Sierra's friends started laughing. "Sierra's on the yearbook committee," said one of them, Carin. "She's always doing stuff like this."

I nodded. "Oh."

Sierra's face brightened. It was stunning to watch. Just a thought careening around inside her brain made her face luminous. "Hey! Wanna help?"

"Help? With what?"

"Yearbook committee. We have no guys." Sierra

glanced around at all her friends. "Just us. We need a guy's perspective on some of the pictures we're choosing."

I tried my best not to look startled. I needed yearbook committee like I needed a hole in the head. But if it meant hanging with these girls, well . . .

"Okay, I'll try it. But only once. Just to see."

"Sure," Sierra said. "After school tomorrow? In the art room?"

"But I have soccer practice. . . ."

"It won't take long. Promise."

4

I dreaded it all day long. Yearbook committee. How in the world had I let myself get dragged into it? I knew what I had to do. One quick look, try to make something good happen with Sierra, and then get out. Never to be seen again.

I'm sure Sierra thought I was looking forward to it. It was probably something she thought was right up there at the top of the Most-Important-Things-in-the-World list. I knew a girl like her had to keep lists like that. My list was a lot smaller.

I dragged it out as long as possible. I took my sweet time dropping books off at my locker after school. I trudged down the hall toward the art room, timing it so I'd have only a few minutes there before I had to head off to soccer practice.

Sierra and all her friends were there when I arrived. And, true enough, there wasn't another male in sight. No guy in his right mind would ever set foot in this place. It was a girl thing.

They were all gathered around a table, looking at a book. I slipped up behind them, put one hand on Sierra's shoulder, and peered down over the top of them. It was easy because I was so much taller than all of them. They were flipping through pictures. Party pictures, group shots. Boring stuff like that.

Sierra glanced at me. "You're here."

"Yeah, I've always wanted to work on yearbook," I lied. Just needed to buy some time.

"Really?" Sierra answered.

I shrugged. "Sure, why not?" I checked out the pictures. They were all group shots, but I recognized one of the guys in a picture—Michael, her old boyfriend, the senior she'd just broken up with.

Sierra was in it too. She was cute in the picture, like a little doll. She was always cute, always dressed to the hilt. Now, then, always. She was wearing a nice dress, one that was cut just right.

She was also wearing shoes that jumped out at you—dark red, with straps around the ankles. They looked very, very expensive. Not my thing. But clearly hers.

I reached over the group, making sure I made casual contact with Sierra. I tapped one of the pictures, the one with Sierra and Michael. "I like this one. It's a good picture of you, Sierra. Great dress, but those shoes are amazing."

degrees of betrayal

Sierra turned, beaming. I must have hit on something. Who knew what? But, hey, if it works. "You do?" she asked.

"Absolutely," I said, nodding. I gave Sierra's shoulder an affectionate squeeze as I pulled back. Whatever floated her boat was fine by me.

We spent a few more minutes sorting through pictures. Sierra was in complete command of her environment. This was her world. These were her people. But I could manage it fine. Give me time, and I could fit in anywhere, anytime. All I needed was a little information.

I had to get to soccer practice. "Sierra?" I whispered in her ear. She turned to face me. "I have to go, sorry."

Sierra glanced over at the rest of the group. "You know . . ."

"Yeah?"

"We're going out tonight, to get some pictures at the baseball field near the water park. We'll probably go mess around with the go-karts after that."

Highview's baseball team had a big district game that night. The field was off-campus, near a water park and a silly little go-kart track.

"Go-karts? You're serious?" I couldn't imagine Sierra in a go-kart. But if everyone else was doing it, then, sure, it made sense.

"I'm serious. But if you don't think you can handle us . . ."

I laughed. "Don't worry. I can handle it."

Sierra turned back to her pictures. "So I'll see ya."

■   ■   ■

Wouldn't you know it? A girl kept cutting me off. It made me crazy. It was that same mousy girl, Kenzie, the one who'd asked me about the goal at the soccer game. She and her driving partner, the Chinese girl, always buzzed in front of me.

I felt like I was being stalked. This girl had no idea what she was doing, but she was smart enough to keep me from getting by her. Every time I looked over one shoulder to spot Sierra, the mousy girl would cut me off.

But I had only one thing in mind. Nothing else mattered. It was like soccer. A fake here, a deception there, a little extra speed when you had space and room. Then go to goal.

I was Sierra's partner by the third time around the small figure-eight track. It wasn't a hard track, just a fun place to hang. The karts were big enough for two to drive. After I'd outmaneuvered all of them the first two times around, Sierra had doubled up with me. She was content to let me drive. And win.

It was nice, sitting next to Sierra. She fit. I was able to steer with my left arm and hold her close with my right. Sierra didn't object. She stayed close.

At some point I checked to see that none of Sierra's friends were worried. You know, about the Korean-American thing. I wasn't white, like all of Sierra's friends. It wasn't anything I thought about anymore. But not everyone was like that. People still worried.

In my own neighborhood, in the 16 square blocks

of the Korean-American community where my parents ran four convenience stores, I never saw anyone like Sierra. I only saw Koreans. Most spoke English. Some did not. It was the way things were.

But I spent as little time as I could in that world. It was my parents' world. It wasn't mine. I had no interest in that place. Almost all the stores had signs in both Korean and English. Some of the translations were moronic. They made sense in Korean. They were a joke in English.

My father's stores didn't make that mistake. He'd been in the States long enough, so he knew. He was comfortable in both worlds. But many were not. Like my mother. She was only comfortable in the Korean world. She was safe there. She never left it.

I made my own place. And because I was taller than the usual Korean-American, because I did what I wanted, played what I wanted, went where I wanted, spoke as I pleased—my world was my own. I always thought it was how you looked at things.

None of Sierra's friends objected. I could tell they approved. I was Sierra's type. I fit too, even though I wasn't white like them. I dressed like them and talked like them. So I fit. It was okay.

But there was one small problem. Sierra was way out of my league. Her family was rich. Mine wasn't. But I could match it. I could keep up. No problem. I always found a way. And I would find a way to stay with Sierra. I had no doubts, none whatsoever.

5

There's a restaurant that only rich white people go to. I think I was one of the few ethnic kids to walk through the door. When I stepped in on Friday night, all I could see was a sea of white pasty faces, all laughing and smiling at how lucky they were to be able to afford to eat dinner at such a place.

I'd asked Sierra out on a real date after the go-karts. Then I'd asked one of Sierra's cheerleader friends, Holly, about the best place to take Sierra on our first date.

"The Lantern, silly." Holly laughed. "I can't believe you even have to ask."

I didn't ask why. I knew why. If I couldn't afford to take Sierra to a place like The Lantern, then I didn't pass the test. There was a threshold to be

crossed. I needed to be able to handle Sierra, and
taking her to a place like The Lantern was just the
appetizer.

I knew I was in deep trouble when I called to
make the reservation. They wouldn't accept it from
me, because I was just a kid. They wanted a commitment that I would show up and that I could pay.

So they asked to speak to one of my parents. I
wasn't about to put my mother on the phone, with
her broken English. So I put Joon, my little sister,
on instead.

Joon may have been two years younger than me,
but she could sound like an adult whenever she
wanted. Oh, who am I kidding? Joon was more of
an adult than I was most of the time. She could stay
with me on anything, anytime. And she was always
ready to try things for me.

"Come on, Joon," I pleaded with her. "Just call."

"You call," she said, refusing to look away from
the silly Disney show she was watching.

Joon drove me nuts sometimes. She was the
most sophisticated kid I knew. She was way beyond
the freshmen kids she was forced to hang around
with. There didn't seem to be anything she couldn't
handle.

She'd already read the Bible through, cover to
cover. Twice. She said she was curious about the
meaning of life. Joon was like that. She went and
found out about things.

I teased her sometimes about her "Christian
thing." But not too much. I'd never tell her this,
but I had to admire the way she went out and found

something to believe in, then fought like crazy
to defend it.

I did stuff. Joon figured it out.

But just when you thought she was this amazing
sophisticated kid able to handle anything, she'd
sit there in front of the TV and watch some stupid
Disney show about magic skateboards. Go figure.

"I can't call," I tried with Joon. "You'd do it
better. You sound like a mom."

"Well, sound like a dad, then," she said, still
refusing to look away from her TV show.

"Joon, please . . ." I let my voice trail off. I knew
Joon would do it. She could never refuse me, even
when she was in a bad mood.

She sighed, hit the "mute" button on the remote,
and finally looked at me. "Okay, so what's the deal
with this girl? Why are you so freaked?"

"I just wanna get it right, that's all," I said.

"So just . . . just go do stuff, like you always do."

"I can't," I said glumly. "I have to take her to The
Lantern."

"Why?"

"'Cause I just have to. All her friends said I have
to take her to The Lantern for the first date. I don't
have a choice."

"And this place is a fancy restaurant, right?"

"Yeah, fancy."

"And expensive?"

"Yeah, expensive." I sighed.

Joon stared at me for a minute. She knew me.
She knew I had no money, not really. My mother
and father both gave us a little allowance money.

It didn't last long. And it sure wouldn't pay for a place like The Lantern.

I could see the questioning look in Joon's eyes. Where would I get the money to pay for this date? But she didn't ask the question. She never did. She knew I'd find a way, somehow. And she never asked me how.

Joon could also see that I wanted to do this. And, in the end, that was all that ever mattered with us. I would do anything for Joon. And I knew, beyond any shadow of a doubt, that there was nothing on earth she wouldn't do for me.

"Get me the phone," she growled.

"Yes!" I said quietly, more to myself than to Joon. But she heard me. She always heard me.

I marveled at the way she handled the call. She made her voice a little deeper than normal, to sound more like a mature woman. She got me the reservation I wanted.

The only thing I forgot to have Joon ask was the cost. But, if they were screening the reservations, then it would take some serious cash to cover the cost of the meal.

Which meant, of course, that I would need to get creative.

My father always keeps his wallet on top of the bureau in their master bedroom. He carries well over $1,000 with him at all times so he can cover cash shortages at any of his four stores.

I had to be careful about it. My mother was around almost all the time, moving from room to room, doing stuff. But there was one time when she didn't budge from one spot in the house—the kitchen, while she was making dinner.

So I waited until she was making dinner and Dad was taking a shower after coming home from work.

I whipped around the corner and bolted into the bedroom. It took me only a moment to find his wallet. I checked to make sure the shower was still running and then rifled through his wallet. I took 10 20-dollar bills and then replaced the wallet exactly as I'd found it. I was back out of the bedroom within seconds.

Sure, it was a risk. But it was an acceptable one. I could raid his wallet like that on a regular basis, but I didn't. Too much risk in that. But one time was probably safe.

There was also the car question. But I felt pretty safe on that one.

My grandparents had given Joon and me $2,500 each when we were very little. I didn't find out until later, but the account had almost doubled by the time I'd gotten to high school.

It was supposed to be for college. But I'd argued and argued with my father about it for months. Finally my club soccer coach had convinced my folks that I was going to get a college scholarship to play soccer.

So my dad gave in. He let me take $2,000 from the fund to buy an old used car. He agreed to pay for the insurance coverage and one tank of gas a week.

Joon had helped me look through the car ads for weeks. Finally we found the right vehicle—an old dark blue Ford Explorer.

It was really old. But the Explorer hadn't changed its appearance in almost a decade. The old ones looked just like the new ones, except with less dents and scrapes.

I kept my Explorer clean, inside and out. It made it look nicer. The Explorer was fine. Not a Bentley, like Sierra's car. But it would do.

As I drove over to Sierra's neighborhood Friday, which felt a lot like driving to another continent—going from the smaller Korean houses to the sprawling mansions near Sierra's house—I changed all the radio presets in my SUV.

I got rid of the hip-hop, alternative, and everything else I always listened to by myself. I set all six stations to light FM rock and that girl-band, silly love-song junk. I hated that stuff. But I knew Sierra would like it. No one had to tell me. She liked mush.

I also knew her mom would meet me at the door. I was ready. I knew she'd freak when she saw me, some big Asian kid who towered over her. Not the little white boys she was used to. I'd need to get her on my side right away.

Joon had helped with my clothes. She picked out the best white boy stuff she could find. I was sharp. I could feel it. I would make an impression.

Sierra's mom and dad answered the door together. Someone must have told them that something unusual had entered Sierra's protected little life.

"Mrs. Reynolds, it's so nice to meet you," I said as the door opened wider. I was getting the max out of my minimal politeness genes. I extended a hand in her mom's direction. Sierra's mom hesitated. It was only a brief pause, the tiniest of hesitations. But it was enough. I knew. I wasn't blind. I saw weakness in others the way a lion senses injury in its prey.

Then she grasped my extended hand with both of hers. "Why, um . . ."

"Ryun, ma'am. Ryun Lee. I'm a junior at High-view, with Sierra. I play for the soccer team. I'm on yearbook committee."

Sierra hopped from around a corner. "Not yet he's not. He has to prove himself."

"I will." I laughed.

I turned my attention back to Sierra's mom. I had to achieve victory here before we left, and I didn't have much time. "Mrs. Reynolds, you must be so proud of Sierra—all of her accomplishments, how respected she is at school." I gave her my most intense gaze.

"Oh, my, yes," her mom said, blushing. And then she looked away.

"It's an honor and a privilege to take her out this evening," I said. "We'll be back early."

Her father nodded soberly. Her mom hesitated again, not sure what she was seeing, in more ways than one. But she nodded too.

"All right, then," I said, opening the door to let Sierra escape. We moved briskly away from her house. I'd won.

"Are you always so polite?" Sierra whispered in my direction so only I could hear.

"Only when absolutely necessary," I answered.

I couldn't take my eyes off Sierra all during

dinner. She had the deepest green eyes I'd ever seen. She was like a postcard . . . really.

I let her do most of the talking during dinner. It was easier that way. Girls can talk and talk and talk. Just turn 'em loose and away they go. Just nod every so often, throw in a "yeah" and a "really?" and a "mmm-hmmm" every once in a while. Sierra was no different—just cuter and smarter and better dressed.

Joon teased me all the time that I got by with my "stare." She said people thought I was smarter than I really was because I pretended to be interested in what they were saying—and didn't offer anything back. She might be right.

Sierra didn't even blink when they brought the menu. She ordered an appetizer—the most expensive one on the list—and then only nibbled when it came out. She ordered sparkling Perrier. I drank the water they offered—for free.

"You know, I can't wait," Sierra said at one point in the conversation, somewhere in between nibbles on her expensive appetizer and nibbles on her even more expensive main course.

"Wait?" I asked, trying not to sound too confused. Sometimes it was better to repeat the question when you weren't sure what was going on.

"Senior year," she said, her voice bouncy. "I can't wait. I know it's going to be the *best!*"

Sierra looked at me with her deep, soulful, green eyes. I could see that she believed it, that she *was* looking forward to her senior year. For her, it would be the best time of her life.

Not me. I wanted to be as close to college as I could my senior year. If I was lucky, I'd get my college scholarship offer some time during the fall of my senior year, and I could coast the rest of the year. Maybe I'd take all my senior year classes pass-fail.

"Me too," I lied. "I can't wait for senior year."

"I mean," Sierra continued to gush, "there isn't anything we can't do when we're seniors. And we have the whole entire year to figure out what we want to do next."

I almost laughed. I knew exactly what I wanted—to get out of the world I was stuck in, with my square parents who worked way too hard, in a community that couldn't see past its nose, and friends who had no idea who I was. I wanted out. Anywhere was better than where I was.

But I never told that to anyone. Joon, maybe, in funny little ways. But definitely not to someone like Sierra. She wouldn't understand, not in a million years.

"So what do you want?" I asked instead.

"To do? Like, with my life?" she asked.

"Yeah, your life. What are you into?" I leaned closer, across the table, and gave her the stare. It wasn't like I cared all that much about the answer. But I had to look like I cared. Didn't I?

I tried hard to keep my eyes from drifting or glazing over, as she told me about yearbook committee, the shoes she'd seen at the mall a day ago, and the horrible dress that some girl had worn to school that day. I did a pretty good job. I was almost certain I had her fooled.

I'm probably being mean. Sierra wasn't a lot different than most girls I knew. She was probably a whole lot smarter and deeper than I was giving her credit for. I had this funny feeling that girls tended to keep their true feelings and thoughts buried way down deep somewhere and only let them out every so often. But it wasn't like I knew for sure.

If I'd been listening and paying attention, I would have known a lot about Sierra's life by the end of the conversation. But I knew enough to get by. I could always bluff the rest.

Sierra had some amazing friends. They were all girls I'd seen and known about since freshman year. Every girl that any guy had an interest in was part of Sierra's world. Every single one. It was like they'd all looked at each other and decided that they were all part of one big club.

And Sierra seemed interested in *me*.

"So what's a big soccer tournament like?" she asked me at one point. "Is it like a Highview game, with everybody cheering for you?"

"It isn't anything like high school," I said, laughing.

"What do you mean?"

I leaned back in my chair. This was something I could talk about. "Well, the teams are all great. They would all kill Highview's team."

"Really?"

"Yeah. And only a few parents watch us now. When we were little, there were lots of parents. But now that we're older, and we all can drive ourselves to the games, there isn't anyone on the sidelines."

"No cheerleaders?"

I grinned. "No cheerleaders. Just a bunch of really good soccer players and the college coaches watching us."

"College coaches?"

"Absolutely." I nodded. "We played in a tournament in Florida this past winter. There were more than 100 college coaches watching our semifinal game against a team from California."

"No way!"

I could see that Sierra was genuinely impressed. She'd had no idea. But, then again, not many did.

Serious sports were no longer played in the high schools. All kinds of sports—like soccer, baseball, basketball, softball, whatever—were played in leagues and tournaments outside the schools. Only football seemed to be a high school thing anymore, and even that was changing.

"Yep," I said confidently. "They were all D-1 schools . . ."

"D-1?"

"Division 1, in the NCAA," I said quickly. "Big schools like Virginia, Wake Forest, Florida State, Georgetown. It's the top level of college sports."

"Oh, I see," Sierra said, nodding. This was definitely not her thing. But she seemed fascinated by it. It was a world she'd never seen before. Like a shiny toy.

I wondered if she looked at me and thought, *I can't believe it. This shallow guy is into some stupid sport where you run around in shorts and kick a ball in front of you.*

But probably not. Sierra was, well, she was just too nice to even think thoughts like that. She probably *was* intrigued with my life.

I tried not to faint when they handed me the check. It wasn't easy. I thought for sure that $200 would be a lot more than I'd need for the dinner. But I was wrong. I could see that it would take a pile of cash to keep up with Sierra.

Even with the $200 I'd taken from my father, I almost didn't have enough. But Sierra would never know. I calculated the tip and then dropped the cash on the check. Cool as ice. I had about 10 bucks left. Appearance is everything. Nothing else matters.

I didn't try to kiss Sierra at the end of our first date. Not that I didn't want to. Oh, did I ever want to. But I also knew her mom was watching as I opened the SUV's door for Sierra and escorted her up the driveway.

Sierra's mom was the type who'd never dream of watching her daughter on one of her other dates, with her usual kind of boy. But she watched me. I knew she'd be watching me. I was sure I'd seen the curtains rustle a little as we pulled up to the front of the house.

I took Sierra's hand as we walked up the driveway. But no kiss. Next time, when her mother wasn't watching. Tonight, right here, I was on my best behavior.

"I had a nice time tonight, Sierra," I said as we got close to the front door.

Sierra turned to face me. There was that smile again, the picture-postcard smile.

It was the kind of smile any guy would fall for, and I knew many guys had. Sierra was the kind of girl you dated because she looked good . . . and that made you look good. But I wasn't sure there was anything else to her other than the window dressing.

"I did too," she told me.

I squeezed her hand, but not too tight. "I'll see you in school. And I'll call you." I let her hand go and took a step backward to let Sierra know I wasn't going to try to kiss her. I was pretty sure she understood.

"Okay," she said, nodding.

I wanted to kiss her. Every part of me ached. But not tonight, not now, not here. Not with her parents right at the other side of the door. She gave a quick wave good-bye, turned, opened the door, and vanished back into her world.

I turned and headed back to mine.

6

When I got back to my Explorer, I pulled out my wallet to check. My fake ID was there. I hadn't forgotten it. I turned all the radio stations back to the way I liked them. No way could I take another girl singer. Not one more love song. I'd had enough.

I played soccer with 25 Korean men every Sunday. Actually, I *toyed* with all of them every Sunday. They were past their prime and out of shape. There was no way they could keep up with a kid like me who trained every day of the week.

They were all in their early 20s and had moved out of the Korean neighborhood years ago. They were lawyers and accountants and stockbrokers and junior executives. They were all on their way up. Not one of them spoke broken English.

And I could take them all. They loved having me on their team because I could take any long ball from the back and score. They got a big kick out of letting me play with them. I liked hanging with them. It was nice. I liked their world. I liked it a lot.

Their favorite place was a dive called the Crow Bar, on the outskirts of the business district. It was at 89th and Lincoln, in a very seedy part of town. The bar was faded and weathered, with these stupid painted crows on the outside. But despite its appearance, it had a steady clientele during the week.

On Friday and Saturday night it was jammed. I could always count on going there and seeing someone I knew. I'd been there so much I was a regular.

My fake ID said I was 22, so it wasn't hard to get into the place. I was big enough, and I looked the age. No one had ever questioned me.

There was something about the Crow Bar that pulled me back, no matter what else I had going on. Maybe it was the fact that I could go there and know there was no way I would ever run into anyone from Highview. It was an absolute guarantee of going to another world, another time.

It didn't hurt that I could sit on a bar stool and stare at real, grown-up women in short skirts and sheer blouses. Girls didn't wear clothes like these women. They might pretend. But these were women, not girls. And I couldn't help myself. I was fascinated.

"Ry!" one of my soccer buddies called out as I came into the Crow Bar. I didn't even need to show my ID anymore. I kept it with me. But they knew me.

"Hey!" I called out to the guy, a lawyer who put in about 100 hours a week at a firm downtown. His only diversions were soccer on Sundays and this bar late in the evening.

"Join us," he said, grabbing another chair and making room at their table.

I settled in. There were four other young men from my Sunday soccer team at the table. "So where ya been?" one of them asked me.

I glanced around to see who was in earshot. It was safe. "I was on a date."

All of them smiled. They loved hearing about my exploits. It took them back to their time in high school.

"Was she cute?" someone else asked.

I smiled. "Yeah, she's cute." I could see Sierra's deep green eyes as I answered. I could even still remember what she smelled like.

"So did ya get some action?" the same guy asked.

"Hey, c'mon." I laughed. "It was a first date. And you all know I'm a good boy."

That cracked them up. They knew better. One of them signaled a waitress and ordered my usual drink—a Dewar's scotch on ice, nothing else.

I pulled the pack of Marlboros from my shirt pocket and smoothly flipped one out, lit it up, enjoyed the long drag and the first nice rush from the nicotine. I kept the cigarettes stashed in the spare wheel compartment of the Explorer and pulled them out when I wasn't around my friends or school.

Girls were all so ditzy, they didn't know. If I'd had a cigarette, I always popped breath mints before I saw any of my dates. And if they smelled it on my clothes, I always said it was from guys who smoke and who I hung around with some. Not my soccer friends. Other unnamed guys. Girls bought it every time.

I didn't smoke too much. I could take it or leave it. I knew it cut into my stamina at soccer, but I could always quit when I needed to. I wasn't hooked. I just liked the things. So sue me.

When the drink arrived, I took my time with the first sip. I loved that first taste, when the whiskey burned and burned on its way down your throat. And then the warmth that settled into your stomach. And, after two more drinks, the light-headedness. I could never get enough of that feeling.

I never worried about drinking too much and then climbing back in the SUV to drive home. I knew I was fine. I was invincible. Nothing could happen to me. It was like my life was on autopilot. I just floated along, experimenting, trying what I wanted, tiptoeing along the edge. It was okay. My balance was perfect. I would never slip.

Joon said I was lucky. Maybe I was. Either way, it all worked.

After two drinks, I could listen to anything these guys wanted to talk about. After two drinks, everything made perfect sense. I simply took it all in, offering a comment only when it was absolutely necessary.

How many kids in high school got to hear this

kind of stuff, anyway? I figured. Not many. So it was homework. For real life.

And when my words slurred, or when my elbow slipped off the table and my drink sloshed and spilled, I didn't notice. I didn't care. It was all good.

7

I wasn't prepared. It wasn't something he usually did.

My father almost always worked late in his office at the other end of the house and didn't see me when I came home from the Crow Bar. But this time he was in the living room.

I tried to slip by before he saw me. It didn't work.

"Son," he called out.

I'd almost made it past the open doorway. Almost, but not quite.

"Yeah, Dad?" I called back. I hesitated. Maybe I could get by with a couple of answers to his questions. I knew it would be tough to carry on a conversation without slurring my words a little. I'd have to be careful.

"Can you come here for a moment?"

I took a deep breath. I shook my head back and

forth several times, trying to clear the cobwebs. I knew my eyes had to be bloodshot, so I'd have to cover that one.

I eased my way around the corner. My father was sitting in a chair. A book was open on his lap.

"Whatcha readin'?" I asked him. I started to rub both of my eyes furiously as I entered the room. I needed to make this good. I didn't stop rubbing them as I walked across the room. I bumped into a chair and almost stumbled.

"A new book on the two Koreas," my father answered in that dead-straight, monotone voice of his. He was always so serious. About everything. He paused and watched me still rubbing my eyes. "Are you all right?"

"My eyes," I said, blinking as I pulled my hands away. "They're killing me."

My father leaned forward and peered at me closely. "I can see that. And that smell? What is it?"

My mind raced. I had to think quickly. "My eyes . . . they're really red, right?" I asked him, buying a little time.

"Yes, they're quite red," my father said, still gazing at me even as he set his book aside and settled back in his chair.

Even here, late at night, in his own home, my father was not relaxed. His collared, knit polo shirt was buttoned all the way to the top. His khaki pants were creased and pressed. He'd probably put them on when he got home from work. He had casual dress shoes on, not slippers. I wondered, sometimes, if he'd ever been . . . normal.

"We had to go to the smoking section of the restaurant," I finally managed. I spoke slowly, choosing each word carefully to make sure one didn't slide into the next. It wasn't easy. But I could manage anything, even this.

"The smoking section?" he asked.

"Yeah, the restaurant was jammed. So we agreed to sit in the smoking section so we didn't have to go some place else."

"I see," he said. "So that's what I smell? Smoke from that section?"

"Yeah."

"And that's all you did on your date?"

"Yeah. We just ate."

"And was your allowance enough to cover it?"

"I'm fine."

"And were you a gentleman? Did you behave yourself properly?"

I stared at my father for a moment. I couldn't tell what he was trying to say. "Like open the car door for her?"

"Yes, of course, that," my father said. He frowned. Something else was on his mind. "But I also meant the other things that a proper young man does . . ."

I could see the way out of this now. "Yeah, Dad, I introduced myself to her parents. I told them a little about me, about our family. I held the door for Sierra on the way out, and I promised her mother that she would be home well in time for their curfew. I'm always a perfect gentleman, just like you've taught me."

I heard an unmistakable muffled snicker from around the corner. Joon was listening in from a safe distance. I was pretty sure my father heard it too, but he chose to ignore it. "Good, then, Ryun," he said, nodding once vigorously. "And, of course, I will presume that you behaved yourself at all times with her."

Man, this was tough. My father and mother had never, not once, had "the talk" with me. And I wasn't about to wade into those waters right now, that was for sure.

"Yes, Dad, I was a perfect gentleman," I said in the most serious tone I could muster. "I walked her back to her house. Her parents were waiting for us when we came home."

My father hesitated. I was pretty sure there was more he wanted to discuss or at least ask me about. But he must have thought better of it because he brought the book back to his lap and opened it again. "Sleep well, Son," he said, dismissing me. "I'll see you at breakfast."

I turned, not too quickly so my head wouldn't spin, and left the room. I started breathing again once I'd left the room and begun to climb the stairs.

"You are *so* lucky!" Joon whispered as I got to the top of the stairs.

"I'm never lucky. Just good," I whispered back. I had a stupid lopsided grin on my face. I never worried around Joon. She would never tell my parents anything, and I didn't worry about her knowing what I'd been doing.

Joon walked beside me on the way to my room. "The smoking section of the restaurant?" she asked, her voice very, very quiet.

"Did ya like that? Good, huh?"

"You know you shouldn't do that stuff, Ry," she said. "For your own good . . ."

I knew Joon couldn't help herself. I would never let anyone else lecture me. But it was okay with Joon, even if she was only a freshman. Actually, I kind of liked it.

Joon lived the straight and narrow. She took the Bible thing seriously. She didn't cuss. She was nice to everyone. She was kind to animals and fat pudgy kids.

And she felt it was her duty to warn me every so often about the dangers and errors of my ways. Not that she was going to change me. That Christian stuff was fine for her. Just not for me. She had her own thing. I had mine.

"You know me," I said casually. "I know my limit."

"Are you sure?" she asked, eyes narrowed.

"I'm sure, Joonie bug." I patted her on the top of the head. "Don't you worry about a thing. I got it all covered."

"But what if something happens?"

"Nothin's going to happen." I leaned against the door to my bedroom. "But thanks for keeping track of me."

Joon smiled. It was a radiant smile. She wanted nothing but happiness for me and asked for nothing in return. "Always," she said, and turned away.

■ ■ ■

The next morning my mother fixed her usual extrav-
agant Saturday morning breakfast. It was the one
day of the week where we could all be together as
a family. No church, no soccer games for me, no
schoolwork.

But, of course, a terrible hangover for me. I
always took four aspirin before bed and still had
this dull headache in the morning. And not much
of an appetite.

I forced myself to eat what my mom put in front
of me. It would kill her if I didn't eat her Saturday
morning breakfast. Just kill her. So I ate. *Slowly.*

"Your father says we have been receiving letters
in the mail," my mother said when we were all
seated.

"Letters?" I asked, confused.

"From colleges," Dad said quickly. "She means
letters from colleges."

"Oh, those," I said. Ever since I'd been picked
for a couple of national Olympic Development team
pools, I'd gotten those letters. And now that I was
a junior, I'd begun to get even more.

Most of them I paid no attention to. I had no
interest in going to schools like smaller Division 1
schools. I wanted an ACC, Big East, Big Ten, or even
a PAC 10 school. Some place like that. My mother
wanted me to go to the best university in the land.
She didn't care about the soccer it offered.

Mom glanced over at Dad. I could see she'd been
thinking about this. "But I have not seen any letters

from those . . ." She stopped. I could see she was struggling for the proper word. But I knew.

"The Ivy League schools?"

"Yes, those," she said. "You have not received any letters from those schools."

It was a question, really. I knew that she understood the answer because we'd been through this before. My mother wanted only the very best for me. She and our father worked very hard to provide for us, and she wanted us—Joon and me—to go to the finest schools in America. She wanted nothing more than that.

"Mom, I've told you," I said quietly. "The Ivy League schools don't offer soccer scholarships. All the other schools do."

"But do you have to play soccer at these schools?" she asked.

I closed my eyes. I had gotten really tired of these kinds of conversations.

"He got a letter from the Duke coach," Joon threw in.

My eyes popped open. I looked over at my little sister. She winked at me.

"I did?" I asked her.

"Yeah, you did," Joon said. She turned to look squarely at Mom. "And you know about Duke, right, Mom?"

My mother tilted her head to one side as she gazed back at her daughter. "No, what is this Duke place?"

"They have one of the best medical schools in the country," Joon said. "*And* one of the best law schools. It looks just like Princeton. It's one of the very best schools in the whole country."

"And it's in the ACC," I added, amazed, as always, at what my little sister knew and seemed to come up with.

"The ACC?" Mom asked.

"It's a big sport conference," I explained. "But that doesn't matter. It's a great school. It would be a great place. And they do offer soccer scholarships there."

My mother looked over at my father. My father nodded. He knew of Duke. It was, in fact, a fine school. And if my father approved, then, well, it would be just fine.

"So you will go to Duke?" my mother asked.

"Mom, it's not quite that simple," I said, trying to keep the pained tone from my voice. "They have to see me play and then offer me a scholarship. . . ."

"And then you can go to this Duke?"

"Yes, and then I can go to Duke," I said.

"Duke has been to two of your tournaments so far," Joon put in.

My *little* sister always surprised me. Of course *I* knew Duke had been there. I'd talked with their assistant coach both times. But I didn't think anyone else in my family knew that. I looked over at Joon. "How do you know?"

Joon shook her head. "You are so . . . so . . ."

"Wonderful, talented, and good-looking?" I said, grinning.

"No, not any of those," she responded. "All you have to do is look up the big tournaments on the

Internet, and they list all of the schools that send
coaches to the tournaments. And I know, for a fact,
that Duke has been to two of them so far."

Wow. Joon was good. "Really?"

"Yeah, really. And I'll bet that, if you ever get
off your duff, put your player bio together, and send
it to them, they'll be interested."

I gave Joon a sideways glance and squinted
one eye. "You wouldn't want to take a shot at that,
would you?"

"Writing your bio?"

"Yeah. I could help, but you're *really* good at that
writing stuff. . . ."

Joon sighed. "You're hopeless."

"So you'll do it?" I pressed. "And send it to Duke
first? So Mom will be happy?"

"Yes, I'll do it," Joon said, shaking her head.

My father cleared his throat. "Good." We all
waited for him to change the subject. "Now, Ryun,
do you have a soccer game tomorrow?"

I shook my head. "No game tomorrow. Why?"

"Because we—your mother and I—would like you
to attend the church service with us. Your sister
comes with us every Sunday. If you do not have
a soccer match, please plan on attending with us.
It is vitally important that you hear the words of
God. . . ."

I looked down at the table. I couldn't believe
my father—or anyone—actually talked like that. Who
in the world talked like that? There was no way I
wanted to go to church with my folks. Maybe with
Joon. I could manage that . . . maybe. But it had

54

been years since I'd been to a church service with my parents.

"I, uh . . . I need to check and make sure Asher hasn't called a practice or something," I said quickly. I knew there was no way that Asher James, my club soccer coach, would call a practice on a Sunday morning. He went to church too.

"But I thought you said you did not have a game?" my father asked.

"No game, but we might have a practice. I just need to check."

"Ryun, we have discussed this many times," my father said in that serious tone of his. "When you do not have soccer, it is very important for you to join us and the other believers in fellowship and—"

"Dad," Joon interrupted as politely as she could manage, "Ryun knows all that. But you know he has soccer almost every Sunday. He has since he was 11." She turned to me. "What Dad means is that it's nice to just talk to other people on Sundays at church about the Bible and stuff like that. It's a chance to get away from school and other things. The sermons are really good."

Bless Joon. She tried so hard to please Mom and Dad. She never seemed to lose patience—or give up, as I had several years ago.

"So check with your coach and see whether you have something, okay?" Joon asked me, her eyes wide. "If not, maybe you can drive me."

"Yeah, that would be good."

"Promise?"

degrees of betrayal

"Yeah, I promise." But I knew that I *would* have something that conflicted with church—whether I really did or not. Though it might not be so bad if I could just go with Joon and skip all the rest.

Someday I'd get a little more serious about the religion thing—if only because Joon cared about it so much. But not now. And definitely not the way my parents wanted me to. There was no way I was headed down that path any time soon.

8

The first time is always the hardest. But once you've done it, and no one jumps out and takes you away, then you know. *I can do this. There are no consequences. Who's to know? Who cares?*

The date at The Lantern had taught me a lot. I needed a boatload of money to keep up with Sierra. She had the nicest clothes at Highview. She spent more at the mall in one weekend than most kids spent in a semester. After Sierra's secondhand Toyota died, her dad had given her an amazing car. A Bentley! Nobody else had a car like that. Nobody.

So I needed a plan. And it sure wasn't going to be some moronic, dead-end job for five bucks an hour. No chance. I would never take a job like that. I'd die first.

There was one place to go. My father. Or, to be

more precise, to one of my father's stores. I had
no choice. It was either go there, or go away
from Sierra. I couldn't ask her to step down. I
had to step up.

My father came here from South Korea in search
of a better way, a better place. He wanted everything for his family. He worked almost around the
clock to make sure we had it—a nice house, nice
cars, opportunities he never had.

When he first came to America, he started with
nothing. He rented out a storefront in the only
Korean neighborhood around at the time and sold
anything that could be sold. After a couple of years,
he opened a second store. By the time I was born,
he'd already opened a third. And soon after Joon
was born, he opened a fourth.

My father spent time at all four stores every
single day. He knew what every employee did at
all four stores. He never took vacations. He worked
seven days a week. It had been years since he'd seen
one of my soccer games. I'd stopped asking him to
come to them a very long time ago. I no longer
cared, either. My father and I simply coexisted,
intersecting only when it was absolutely necessary.
Like trying to make me go to his church or walk the
straight and narrow with my dates.

If you asked my father, he'd say he was doing it
for us—for Joon and me, for our family. But I knew
better. He did it for him.

My father was *something* in the tight-knit
Korean community that somehow managed to cram
an entire world into a few city blocks. He was the

center of their world, not ours. He was their pro-
vider. And if we got something out of that, great.
That was just the way it was.

My mother kept the books for all four stores.
She had an office at one of them, but mostly she
kept track of the money from our home. Every
night, like clockwork, four of my father's employees, one from each of the four stores, would bring
the money—all cash—by the house. My mother
would double-check their figures inside the bags
against her own figures.

My mother, even after all these years, still spoke
only broken English. So around home, we spoke
Korean. My mother paid attention to my father, to
Joon and me, and to the books, in that order. There
was no other world but that. We lived on a small
deserted island in the midst of the real world.

She kept all the numbers on one computer at
home, logged the entries, and printed out deposit
slips for the bank first thing each morning. Every
single night she did it exactly the same way, at
exactly the same time. I knew the routine by heart.
So did my sister.

But I also knew that one of the employees always
printed up the day's take on a hand calculator at the
store. He never wrote the figures by hand. He ran the
numbers on the calculator and put that record inside
the bags with the money collected.

The curious thing, I'd discovered, was that he
didn't keep an account at the store. He simply cal-
culated the receipts, printed them out, and put them
in the bags. He knew my mother kept an exact

accounting herself, so I guess he felt no need to duplicate her efforts.

I watched the process for a while to make sure there were no other records. There were none. There was only his printout each day and an accounting record on my mother's computer at our home.

What's more, the numbers were always about the same each day, give or take a couple hundred dollars on a few thousand dollars' gross. Sometimes a little more, sometimes a little less. They never varied much. You could pick a number, somewhere in the ballpark, and it wouldn't be out of the ordinary.

On Sunday, when my family was off at church, I went to an office supply store and bought the exact same hand calculator. When I got back to the house, I printed up bogus account sheets with different amounts.

Now I had to wait for the right moment during the week when I could intercept a delivery at the front door, exchange one of my accounting sheets that was several hundred dollars less than what he'd actually taken in, lift the cash, and make the switch.

I practiced the run on Monday, just to make sure I could handle it, and then got ready for action. Sure enough, on Tuesday, the kid from one of my father's stores who dropped off a bag of cash had an amount that was slightly higher than one of the preprinted account sheets.

I was so nervous when I peeked inside the bag and saw an amount that was $267 higher than one of my preprinted sheets that I dropped the bag. Some of the money spilled out. My mother called out from the kitchen to make sure everything was all right. I almost aborted the mission right there.

But my mother didn't check up on me, so I went ahead. I bolted to the small office where my mother always counted the money and logged in the cash receipts. I closed and locked the door behind me to make sure no one came in while I was making the switch. Then I counted out $267 as fast as I could, switched the receipts, and dropped the bag next to her computer with the others. I stuffed the $267 into my pocket and left her office as casually as I could. No problem. I was all set.

Except I bumped into Joon as I turned the corner. She gave me a strange look, like she *knew* what I was up to. But there was no way she could have known. And this was not something I would ever share with her. Joon could forgive a lot—but not this.

I practically held my breath for the next two hours. But I didn't need to worry. When my mother checked the money later that evening, when she was done with all of her housework and turned to the books, she had my sheet, which matched what was in the bag. She entered her numbers, turned off the computer, and went about her business as she always did. No problem.

It was neat. Tidy. Flawless. And a guaranteed steady income so I could support Sierra the way that I wanted.

Was this wrong? Yeah, right. Only losers ask that question. It's only wrong if you get caught. And I don't get caught, not at this kind of child's play.

Asher knew.

"Yeah, I know Duke's top assistant coach," he told me at club soccer practice that week. Asher got to practice a half hour before everyone else did. Except me. And I got there early just to hang with Asher and kick the ball around.

"You do?" I asked, surprised.

"Yeah, I do, and I'll make you a deal," he said, his eyes flashing. "Make sure we win State Cup this year, and I'll make sure the guy is at regionals to watch. His name is Johnny Moser, and I've worked with him in the past on a couple of kids."

Asher James was the best coach I'd ever had. He'd been my mentor, friend—and my coach—for years. He'd taught me every move I made on the soccer field. He'd helped me understand the entire game, not just the parts where I had the ball at my foot. He'd allowed me to see everything from a bigger stage.

I should have known he'd know somebody from Duke, but it still surprised me. There was a lot about Asher that still surprised me.

"We'll win State Cup," I vowed. "Don't worry. I'll take care of it personally."

The funny thing was that Asher believed me. Actually, he believed *in* me. If it had to do with soccer, I knew Asher was sure I could handle it.

"So is it true?" he asked me as we kicked the ball around.

"What?"

"That girl. What's her name—Sierra?"

I almost blushed. I never could quite figure out how Asher heard about this kind of stuff. But he always heard. He always knew.

"What about her?" I said. I kicked the ball viciously back at him.

Asher trapped it perfectly, effortlessly, even with the fast speed on the ball. "Oh, nothin'. Just curious, that's all. She doesn't seem your type."

"And what is my type, exactly?"

Asher laughed. "Oh, I don't know. But from what I've heard of this girl, she's not it."

"And what *have* you heard?"

"That she's rich, cool, and great looking. Basically out of your league."

"Yeah?"

"Yeah. It's got to be a pity date. You know, to give the ugly dweeby guy a break . . ."

I kicked a wicked curving ball as hard as I could muster right at Asher's chin. He didn't even blink. He popped up off the ground about a foot or so, trapped the ball with his chest, and then, as the ball was descending, one-touched a rocket back in my direction. It whacked me in the leg before I could even react.

"Hey!" I said. "That hurt!"

"You're slow today," Asher chided. "That girl—Sierra—must have dulled your senses."

I ambled over to get the ball. "So do you really think she's not my type?"

Asher didn't answer right away. He could see that I was serious. "Ryun, I don't think there's anyone—or anything—that's out of your reach on this planet. Not one single thing. But that's almost a curse for you instead of a blessing."

I cracked the ball back to him, planting my left foot next to the soccer ball as Asher had taught me from the time I was little. "Huh?"

"I mean," he said slowly, "that you go a little too fast sometimes because you want everything right away. And you're smart enough to get most of those things that you go after."

"And that's bad?"

"No, not bad. Just dangerous sometimes. I've said it a million times. You aren't invincible . . . even if it seems otherwise."

Asher got like this on me sometimes. Kind of like a grown-up version of Joon. I didn't mind it, really. I knew he had only my best interests at heart. There were no hidden agendas with Asher James. He wasn't trying to make a career off me. He'd had his career, and he was only giving me what he knew. But he sure could get preachy every once in a while, if I didn't slow him down.

"Okay, I get it," I mumbled. "But Sierra's a nice girl. I'm sure my parents would approve, if they cared about it at all."

Asher sighed. "You know, you might be surprised."

"About what?"

"About how much your parents care about you, the girls you date, your soccer ambitions."

"Yeah, right. My dad's been to see, what, maybe three of my matches in the past four years? He cares?"

"Yes, Ryun, he cares," Asher said, stopping the ball and holding it under one foot. "He calls me more than I think you know, and we go over things. He's paying attention, even if he's too busy with work to be here more often."

I shook my head. It wasn't that I didn't believe Asher. But I just didn't see that in my father. So I found it hard to believe he cared as much as Asher said he did.

"If you say so," I said, wanting to change the subject.

"So State Cup? A done deal?" Asher said. "And I talk to Moser?"

"Definitely." I nodded once. "Put it in the bank."

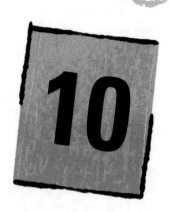

There is only one rule in soccer: Score one more goal than your opponent. There is no other rule, really. Teams can play pretty soccer. They can pass and move with style and flair. They can fake and juke and beat every midfielder. They can take runs at defenders and sail balls over and around the post all day.

But the prettiest teams don't always win. The best teams don't always win in soccer. If a team packs in nine defenders behind the ball and then launches even one successful counterattack and scores, it can win 1-0.

My club team was a lot like that. They packed in their defense behind the ball and hoped for that counterattack. They had just one superstar. Me. I was their guy. I'm not shy about saying so. I don't make

a big deal about it, but I sure don't walk away from
it, either.

I held up my end of the deal with Asher. We won
our state championship that spring and played for
the regional championship toward the end of July.
And Asher held up his end. He spoke to Duke's
assistant coach, Johnny Moser, who said he'd be
there at regionals to watch me play.

At the regional championships, we played about
a dozen of the other teams that had won their state
titles. Some of them were great. Others were just
pretty good, like our team.

We got lucky. In the group play, where they
randomly assign teams to play each other, our team
drew three relatively weak teams. We got out of the
group and had a chance to play for the regional title.
We got through our semifinal match in a 1-1 game
and won it in a penalty kick shoot-out. I scored the
only goal in that game, with about 100 college
coaches watching.

By the time of the regional final, every college
coach on the grounds was there. We were in our
U-17 year, the time when colleges all start paying
attention. And this tournament was one of the big
ones. It mattered. Guys got full rides coming out of
this tournament.

And I'd had a great tournament. I'd converted
every chance the opposing teams had given me.
When I got the ball, it usually took three defenders
to stop me. The buzz at the place was that I was
unstoppable, unless you trapped me with multiple
defenders.

On a great team, that would be death. With so many defenders on me, it left others open. But we didn't have a great team. There was just me, and I had to score by going around or through what the other team threw at me.

In the regional final, they put three defenders on me the entire match. Every time they played the ball long, I had a defender 20 yards deep on me and another right on me. But even with that, I still created at least a half dozen chances in the match.

With 10 minutes to go and the score still tied 0-0, I trapped a long pass up to me with my chest, kicked it out wide as I let it drop to my left, and then sprinted for the flag as fast as I could. The deep defender went with me. I left the other defender in the dust.

But the instant I crossed the corner of the 18, I reversed direction and cut the ball back. I started to race across the top of the box, parallel to the goalkeeper.

As I got clear of the last defender—and I had only a split second to make the decision—I launched a rocket with my left foot toward the near post.

It was the hardest move and shot in soccer—going to your left, then shooting the ball with your left foot back toward the post of the goal you were racing away from.

It caught the goalkeeper by surprise. He was moving with me, so when the ball went back in the other direction, it slipped into the side of the net. My teammates mobbed me.

Ten frantic minutes later we were the regional

champs. There were hundreds of people watching, shouting, clapping. It was crazy. Sometimes it gets like that at soccer matches. Not at many in America, but at some of them. This was one of them.

At that moment, more than any other moment I'd ever known, I believed there was nothing at all on this earth that I could not conquer, could not achieve, could not have if I wanted it. It was the most amazing feeling, unlike any other I could imagine.

It also secured any college scholarship I wanted. I knew for a fact that every one of my target schools had seen me score that goal in the middle of a huge pressure match. I just had to decide.

But I was now set on going to Duke. Joon had put the thought there, and it would make my mother and father happy. So Duke University it was.

Duke had one of the better college soccer programs around, and I sure couldn't afford the 30K a year in tuition. Without a soccer scholarship, there was no way I could go to a school like Duke.

So even as we were in the middle of our celebration, I took one quick look at the sideline, just to make sure.

And he was there—Johnny Moser, the young, scruffy-looking assistant coach with the buzz cut who always wore a Duke basketball jersey to these things and who'd been to see me twice before at big tournaments in the spring. Our eyes met. He gave me a quiet salute, letting me know that he'd seen. And approved.

"Great goal," he said. I could read the words on his lips even from here.

"Thanks," I answered silently.

Even Sierra knew him. She'd been with me at both of the other tournaments where I'd bumped into Moser. Sierra always stood quietly at one corner of the field, near the spots where the coaches always watched with their clipboards. Sierra never stood near the parents.

She had listened in on one of my conversations that spring with Moser after Asher had spoken to him. She hadn't said anything, but I could see she was impressed that a coach from a school like Duke paid so much attention to me.

So it was done, if I wanted it. Duke was mine for the asking. Moser would make sure of it now after this performance. It didn't matter that we'd get killed at nationals, probably finish dead last. We'd won here, and I'd delivered. Duke knew what I was capable of handling. That was what mattered. At least to me.

Am I arrogant and conceited? Am I? Yeah, I guess I am. But my friends don't know, and my parents don't, either. No one at school has a clue. My teammates don't know because I always seem to help them, not the other way around. Sierra sure doesn't know. I don't talk big. I just act big.

And that's the difference. You'd have to be God to know how I feel about myself, the way I look at the world, the way I take what I want. But God has never made an appearance on my stage, not that I can tell. I'm making it on my own, with no help from anyone else.

And if I knew God was watching? If I knew God was paying attention to me—to me personally, my actions and secret thoughts—would I care? Yeah, I guess I'd have no choice. I'd have to care. I mean, who wouldn't? Then your life would have real meaning, if God was actually paying attention to what you did each day.

There's a certain freedom in believing that God—and everyone else—isn't paying any attention to what you're doing. And a certain gut-wrenching fear too because then you're totally on your own on this planet. But the freedom to do what you want—believing that the only consequence is getting caught—had always won out with me.

Where's the harm in this? Who was I hurting? The soccer team got what they needed from me. So did my friends. So did Sierra. I got good grades, my family thought I was doing everything their way—the right way. They didn't seem all that interested in going a whole lot deeper than that. It was like everybody wanted to live life on the surface, when I wanted to live life on the edge.

So if, along the way, I did my own thing, who was going to tell me something different? It's not like there was anyone—or anything—lurking out there, ready to cast me into some pit of doom and despair.

11

"No way!"

It was scary. Holly and Sierra shrieked at almost the same time. They didn't care who saw them on display in the middle of the crowded mall. They had seen their holy grail, and there was nothing— and no one—to stop them from letting the world know their joy.

"There's just one!" Holly said.

"Hurry!" Sierra said. She left my side in an instant, followed closely by Holly. They vanished into the store within seconds, leaving me behind. And very, very confused.

I glanced around. Several adults glared my way. The outburst had been so sudden, it had startled anybody close to us.

But less than 100 feet away, I saw a group of

young girls—a few years younger than Sierra and Holly—turn on their heels and start to walk very quickly toward me. *What's the deal? Is there some hidden secret signal I'm totally clueless about?* I wondered.

I looked back at the window of the exclusive designer shoe store Holly and Sierra had dragged me to. The price tags on the shoes gave me cold sweats. Most were in the $400 range. At least two of them were almost $700.

Are you kidding me? Almost $700 for a pair of *shoes?* Who would be stupid enough to be interested in a pair of shoes like that?

The group of girls who surrounded me in a matter of seconds, that's who. Within moments there were at least half a dozen girls with their noses pressed up against the window, studying the shoes Holly and Sierra had spotted.

"No way!" one of them said, echoing the exact same words Sierra had shrieked just moments earlier.

I peered over their shoulders at the shoes they were all staring at. I had a tough time making out the name, but I finally managed. Dolce & Gabbana. What in the world was a Dolce & Gabbana, and why did such a flimsy pair of shoes cost almost $700?

I got a little closer. I could see the brands of the other shoes in the window. Isaac Mizrahi, Versace, Anne Klein. The only name I recognized was Kenneth Cole. Every pair was at least $400. Unbelievable.

But, you know, who was I kidding? In my own little world, people paid ridiculous prices for soccer shoes all the time. It wasn't all that unusual for a 12-year-old kid who was really into soccer to demand that his parents shell out $200 for a pair of Adidas Predators. It happened all the time.

Not me, of course. I knew better. I had long ago learned how to find knockoffs for about a third of the price through soccer warehouses. But I understood the principle. Status came with what you wore on your foot. The more expensive, the more important you were supposed to be. That was the theory, at least.

There is an unspoken rule in sports. If you are going to wear flashy shoes, you'd better be *really* good. Because everyone is going to notice you. If you're a big goof and fall on your face with those flashy shoes, you will never live it down.

Somewhere in my brain a thought was beginning to register. If a girl is going to wear expensive designer shoes, she'd better be able to justify it. She'd better be the real thing.

Well, Sierra *was* the real thing. She could handle the $700 Dolce & Gabbanas in the window. I glanced at the gaggle of young girls with their noses pressed up against the show window near me. They were maybe 13 or 14. They couldn't handle the Dolce & Gabbanas. At least, not yet. But maybe someday—with a girl like Sierra showing them how to manage it.

An instant later Sierra showed up on the other side of the window, inside the store. Our eyes met. She gave me a secretive knowing glance. She reached down and plucked the pair of $700

Dolce & Gabbanas from the window, showed them
to me for my approval. I nodded once back at her.
She turned and signaled a store clerk.

The young girls on the other side of the window
all turned toward me as one. Their eyes were wide
with a mixture of excitement and curiosity.

"Will she buy a pair of Dolce & Gabbanas?"
one of the girls asked me.

"She might," I answered. "If she likes them."

All of the girls turned back, their eyes riveted
on Sierra. They watched and cataloged her every
move—how she carried herself, how she discussed
the shoes so casually and confidently with the store
clerk, how it was no big deal at all that she was
about to try on a pair of $700 Dolce & Gabbanas.
It was breathtaking.

I couldn't help myself. This was poetry in motion,
unlike anything I'd ever known or experienced
before. This was a world so far removed from mine
that I felt like a distant alien observing unknown life
forms for the first time.

The girl who'd first addressed me turned back.
"Is she your . . . ?" she asked, leaving the question
hanging.

"My girlfriend?"

"Yeah," the girl answered.

I smiled. It was nice, hearing that question. "Yes,
Sierra is my girlfriend."

"Wow, she's so pretty," the girl said and then
turned back to look inside.

It was so weird how girls knew that about other
girls. They knew who was pretty. And the pretty

ones, like Sierra, in some mysterious way, showed other girls how to be just a little prettier, cooler, and more stylish along the way. It was way beyond me how all this happened.

I decided to join the fashion rock star onstage and headed into the store. I took a seat next to Sierra, on the other side from Holly, and glanced back out toward the girls who were still staring through the window.

Sierra glanced at me, then back out the store to the young girls watching. She smiled at me, her green eyes sparkling. I could tell she was happy I was here with her, taking part in her own little drama.

"So what do you think?" she asked.

"Of the shoes? The Dolce & Gabbanas?"

Sierra gave me a startled look. "You know about Dolce & Gabbana?"

"You never know about me," I said, laughing. I wasn't about to tell her that I'd just heard about the shoes a few minutes earlier from a girl younger than my sister. Better to let Sierra guess.

The clerk brought two different sizes back. I couldn't help but admire how gracefully Sierra tried them on. She was so delicate in how she undid the clasp and slipped the shoes on. And when she stood up and walked around the store with them on, I could almost hear the collective gasp from the young girls outside the store.

There was no question. Sierra *was* the real thing. Somewhere, in some distant corner of the world, there was a shoe designer. And when he designed a shoe such as this, he had a girl—a young woman—like Sierra in his mind.

The elegance and grace of Sierra and the shoes were almost one and the same. And if someone like me could see it, then there was some sort of order to the world that I hadn't seen before.

"Wow, she looks great in those, doesn't she?" Holly whispered to me as Sierra continued to walk around the store in the shoes.

"Yeah, she does," I said, unable to contain my sense of awe. "Sierra's amazing in those shoes."

Holly glanced over at me. I think she was surprised that I got it too. "Yes, she is," she answered and turned her attention back to Sierra.

I looked back through the window. Every girl watched Sierra as closely as the distance would allow. Every step, every movement Sierra took was captured.

I could now see what Sierra always liked to talk about. Making memories. These girls would take away this memory as they thought about the shoes they'd wear to homecoming or their wedding. Sierra's grace and elegance would be that memory . . . and guide.

"She won't actually buy the shoes, though, will she?" I whispered back to Holly.

Holly tilted her head. "You never know with Sierra. She might. But probably not. I think she just wanted to see what they looked like on her."

Sierra took the seat next to me. She leaned very close, putting her hand on my arm. "How do they look?" she asked.

I leaned close too and whispered in her ear, "On you, they look great. Like they were made for you."

Sierra squeezed my arm. That was all she needed to hear. Nothing else mattered. "You're the best," she whispered back. "Thanks."

But in the end, Sierra didn't buy the shoes. She spent a few minutes discussing the price with the clerk to make sure he didn't feel slighted for taking time to let her try the shoes on, then decided to leave the store with only the memory.

But, you know, in some ways that was enough. For everyone who'd taken part. Me too.

"You shouldn't do it."

"Why?"

"Because it's wrong," my little sister said in a very quiet voice. She was quiet in our house, especially when she spoke to me. She always made sure my mother didn't hear what she said to me. She didn't have to worry about my father. He was never around anyway.

"So? Do I care? I don't. You know that."

My sister was two years younger than me and small, like my mother. But she could keep up. She never backed down with me, not like others.

She pursed her lips and flipped her soft black hair over to one side. She gripped her left elbow with her right hand and glared at me through her narrow-set eyes.

Joon's eyes were definitely Korean. And now that she'd begun to wear mascara, her eyes were defined even more. She could look right through me with those eyes.

But I didn't care. My sister would never let on, not to anyone, ever, for any price on earth. She knew me. She knew my soul, and she would die for me. I knew that as surely as I knew anything. Maybe it was the *only* thing I'd ever known for certain.

Joon would always be there, no matter what. Even when I'd given her grief for falling for "the Christian thing" a year ago, about the same time I'd bought the Yamaha and started hanging out at the Crow Bar, she'd never given up on me. She'd just become more stubborn about pointing me back to what she called "the right track" in life.

"But you're already going to Duke. You said so . . ."

"Yeah, but I get five free recruiting trips. And Charlottesville is a great party campus." I didn't finish the rest of the thought. Joon knew.

"Sierra likes you. A *lot,*" she said in the quiet tone she always used when she desperately wanted to convince me of something. Right now she was trying to convince me that it would be a good idea to take Sierra with me on a college recruiting trip.

"Yeah? So? I like Sierra. She likes me. But that doesn't mean . . ."

"Yes, it does," my sister insisted. "What would you think if you found out Sierra was about to meet up with some college guy in a bar somewhere?"

I laughed. "Like that's going to happen."

Sierra and I had been a *thing* at Highview for the rest of our junior year and right through the end of summer. She'd been by my side or near me on and off at school. We saw each other every Friday and Saturday night. She'd driven to all of my away tournaments with my club soccer team. She'd seen all of the college coaches recruiting me.

And during the summer break, we'd been inseparable, for the most part. At least Sierra thought we were inseparable. She had no idea what I did when I was away from her. None. She was clueless. Which was fine.

I was gone a lot during the summer, away at college soccer showcases and tournaments. And I was at practices a lot too, in different parts of the city. My club team traveled a lot. We were out of town all the time.

Coming out of the regionals, I'd locked Duke up. Actually, Asher had mostly locked Duke up with Johnny Moser. But I was still going through the motions, looking at other schools—Maryland, William and Mary, the University of Virginia, UConn, Seton Hall, Stanford, Creighton, Portland, Indiana University, UCLA, and a handful of others. All the top Division 1 soccer schools were interested.

I was an impact player. That meant I could step on the field as a freshman, in the first year, and have an impact on the field. I knew it. They knew it.

College soccer coaches close in for the kill in August, before the senior year of the big-time recruits. They nail down their top picks in September and October, just as their own seasons are under way. They use official visits during the first few games to lock it down.

I knew I was probably headed to Duke. But that wasn't about to stop me from official visits to Virginia, UNC, and a couple of other places. I was taking everything everyone wanted to give me. And then some.

I had an official recruiting trip lined up every weekend from mid-August through the first two weeks of September. The University of Virginia was first on my list, before school started. The students weren't there, but all of the athletes were, for pre-season training.

It was killing Sierra, because she wanted to come along. She thought it made sense, since she was my girlfriend. It didn't. Going to soccer tournaments with me was one thing. Going with me on these college recruiting trips was something else.

Joon knew, of course. She knew exactly what I was doing when I was away at these trips. I already looked 21. So why not complete the assignment? Who could I be hurting?

"You could take her car," Joon said, trying it from another direction.

I smiled. My sister's smart, but I know all her tricks. "Yeah, but she'd still be there with me. I mean, I like the car, but . . ."

Joon sighed. "Sierra's really nice. Why don't you take her with you to Virginia this weekend? Be nice for a change?"

I twirled my SUV keys around my index finger, catching them in the palm of my hand. Then I twirled the keys again, letting them snap loudly into my palm. I was going to Virginia—alone. Nothing my sister could say would change that.

"No chance," I said. "It's hopeless. You won't convince me, so you might as well give up."

"But . . ."

I held up one finger, urging her to be quiet. It was done. "Okay?"

"Okay," she said, casting her eyes downward. "But will you be careful, at least?"

I knew Joon. She was probably saying a prayer for me at that very moment. Which was fine. I might not believe the way she did, but that didn't mean I was ungrateful for the way Joon looked after me.

"Always," I said, laughing. "You know me."

Of all places. Go figure.

After my escort in Charlottesville, Virginia—Billy Smithson, a senior on the University of Virginia men's soccer team—picked me up at the gym, we drove in his car to a dorm to pick up a girl. Inside, I groaned. It was bad enough to have an escort. Now I was going to get stuck with some dog-ugly girl for the night too?

But the girl who walked out toward the car was anything but ugly.

"Ryun, this is Kenzie," Billy said.

She smiled and nodded as she got into the car.

"How's soccer going this summer?" she asked me, as if she already knew me.

I was startled. How did she know I was an athlete? I wondered. For the life of me, I had no clue who she was. I didn't think I'd ever seen her before.

"It's going fine," I said, and stared at her stupidly.

She held out her hand. "McKenzie Parker? From Highview? Everyone calls me Kenzie?"

I shook it and continued to stare. This was McKenzie Parker? No way.

The girl must have known I was still stumped, so she added, "We were at some yearbook committee meetings together?"

I nodded, as if, of course, I knew. But the Kenzie in the car with me looked so different than the mousy girl I barely remembered. She was fit and tan, like she played a sport. She had streaky blonde hair that really complemented her eyes. And she was wearing a great two-piece sundress that showed off her figure. I couldn't believe this was the same McKenzie.

"I can't believe we ran into each other here," Kenzie said as we pulled away from the curb.

"I know," I agreed. "It's too weird." And it was— I run into a girl from *Highview* on a recruiting trip in Virginia? If I believed in things like fate or destiny, I would have been worried. But I don't, so it was just weird.

I guess they put us together because we were both down here on our own, looking at the campus. I had to have an escort because I was on an official recruiting trip. But she must have asked for an escort, so they put us together.

I looked at her and smiled. "But it's nice."

As we sat in the backseat of our escort's car,

I couldn't help but stare more at this new Kenzie.
I tried not to be obvious, but I think she knew.

So much for our tour of the campus. I don't think
either of us could have found our way around if we
were on our own.

At that minute Kenzie scrunched her face up.
"I mean, it's so strange. Sierra and I have been
spending a lot more time together, and now to see
you . . ."

I looked over at Kenzie. "You know Sierra?"

"Well, kind of," Kenzie said. "We're friends, but
not best friends. I know Holly a lot better. We just
got back from summer camp together. We've been
hanging out with Sierra more, though, since camp.
Then Holly left on vacation with her family, so
Sierra and I have been doing stuff. . . ."

"Oh." At first I thought that was a little weird.
Why hadn't I run into Kenzie this summer then?
But Sierra never talked about her friends much
with me. And I never cared all that much, either.
When I was with Sierra, I paid attention only to her
and not much else—even if we were in a crowd.

Kenzie smiled. "Sierra talks about you all the
time. She's always talking about you. About everything."

Kenzie was sitting as far away from me as she
could manage. She was practically hugging the armrest on the other side of the car. So I deliberately slid
over a little, toward her, just to see what she would
do. "Yeah, Sierra can sure talk."

"What's she like when she's around her friends?"

"Sierra?" I asked, surprised by the question.

"Yeah, I mean, I know she has her cheerleading friends and yearbook committee. And everybody seems to love her. But I was wondering . . ."

"If she has other real friends? Yeah, she has other friends. But she hangs with Holly and Carin and the others a lot. I see them all the time when I'm with Sierra."

Kenzie nodded, as if making a mental note. I thought it was funny. I didn't care who Sierra hung out with. But this girl cared. I guess most girls cared about stuff like that. It was their thing—who hung out together, who talked to each other.

"So are you thinking about Virginia?" I asked Kenzie.

"Maybe. It's a good school. I know some kids who go here."

"Me too."

"So what about you?"

I glanced up toward the front of the car. I could see that the escort was listening to our conversation, so I lied. "Yeah, I'm thinking about it real seriously. This was where Bruce Arena got his start, where it all happened. They had a sort of soccer dynasty here for a while."

"Bruce Arena?"

"Yeah, he was Virginia's soccer coach here, before he became a coach with D.C. United and then the World Cup team."

Kenzie nodded politely. "I see."

"Anyway, yeah, I'm thinking about Virginia. Klockner's a great place to play games."

But for some reason I could tell that Kenzie

wasn't buying my lines. She gave me this funny
little smile and then a slight nod toward our escort.

After our escort finished up the tour, we headed
to Klockner Stadium, where the soccer team played.
Then we were going to visit some of the academic
buildings before heading over to a party with a
bunch of the athletes at our escort's fraternity house.

As we walked into Klockner later on the trip,
I couldn't help myself. I mean, soccer's my life.
I could, in fact, see myself playing out there.
Klockner wouldn't be a bad place to play soccer.
I could see myself carrying the ball forward in this
stadium.

Kenzie caught me staring at the pillars that
surrounded Klockner. "Just like Rome, isn't it?"

"Rome?"

"Yeah, the pillars," she said, laughing. "Like
ancient Rome. And you're about to enter the
arena . . ."

"To face the lions." I laughed too.

I liked the way Kenzie seemed to go with the
flow. I liked being here at Klockner, so Kenzie
seemed to like it too. I got the feeling she simply
wanted to be part of something, even if it was
someone else's something.

"So are you serious?"

"About Virginia?" I asked. "Playing here?"

Kenzie glanced over at our escort. She wanted
to make sure we were far enough away so we
couldn't be overheard.

"Yeah. Are you really interested in the place,
or are you just here for a free tour?" she asked.

I glanced over at our escort too. "Just curious, I guess. I mostly like Duke. But it can't hurt to check other places out." *And other girls too,* I couldn't help thinking.

Kenzie nodded. I could see she got it. "I like Virginia. I'd love to go here. But I have to get in fair and square. Soccer won't get me in any place. Not like you."

If somebody else had made that comment, I might have been offended. But Kenzie didn't seem jealous that my soccer could get me into a school like Virginia or Duke. Far from it. Kenzie seemed intrigued—not jealous at all.

"Virginia's okay, I guess. But it might be nice to get out of Virginia for college."

Kenzie laughed again. "Yeah, I'm with you there. I can't wait for the day when I can go away to school and I won't have to babysit my family any-more."

As the day wore on, I found myself growing more comfortable with Kenzie with every conversation, every passing glance, every friendly gesture. It was easy to be with Kenzie. She was grounded, mature, in a way that Sierra was not. I couldn't believe that I'd never noticed her much around Highview before. Where had she been?

I was surprised how honest she was—how fast she put her cards on the table.

"My mom directs a day-care center called Little Lambs," she told me, "and I help out a lot. I really love the kids there. I'm teaching one of them to play the guitar. He's only seven, but he's so smart. . . ."

"Little Lambs?"

"A Christian day-care center," Kenzie explained. "I really like it there. I like putting my faith into action—"

"You're into that?" I interrupted.

Kenzie looked down for a second. But she didn't back down. Good for her. "Yeah, I read the Bible. I go to church. And, yeah, I'm into that. I believe in Jesus, if that's what you mean."

I nodded. "My little sister's like you. Into the Christian thing, I mean. It's okay. I don't mind. People can believe what they want."

I could see this kind of talk made Kenzie uncomfortable. But she stuck with it. And as she talked and let me into her world, I could see her relax.

Kenzie had always led such a cautious sheltered life . . . until this summer.

"I guess, until this summer, I didn't get out much." She laughed. "Since Mom's so busy with the center, I spend a lot of time driving my younger sister and twin brothers around, to games and stuff."

It didn't take long for me to figure out what was going on. "So you're the good girl. You're the second mom. The girl everybody counts on."

"That's me," Kenzie said, just a trace of sadness in her voice.

"And somewhere along the way, you got a little sick and tired of it, right?"

"Right," she said, nodding.

"So this summer . . . ?"

"I decided to try some different things."

I couldn't blame her. I thought back to what

Mom and Dad always talked about—"upholding the family honor." Sometimes those words were like a chain around my feet.

"Yeah, I know the feeling," I said. "I get tired of all that stuff in the family too. It's my life. Why can't my family just leave me alone, let me live my life the way I want to? It's not like I'm hurting them."

"Exactly!" Kenzie said. "My parents couldn't understand why I had to come here this weekend by myself, without them. They didn't get it."

"Really? They wanted to come with you?"

"Yeah, but I needed the time alone. Lark—that's my sister—was pretty ticked, because she wanted to come. But for once I wanted to be on my own. And to do something that only belonged to me. You know?"

I nodded. I did know. It's what drew me to the Yamaha and my ride through the pipe again and again.

"You know, Sierra would never get this," I said, "but there are times when you *have* to go out there on your own. No group. Nobody else. Just you. Figure it out on your own . . ."

"You're right. Sierra would never get that. She always has to have a group around. I don't think she ever spends any time alone."

It was weird. How the two of us connected. I mean, really connected—and in a way that Sierra and I never had.

By the time we got to the frat party, it was obvious.

"Let's ditch Billy," I said to Kenzie. "He doesn't want to hang around with a couple of kids from high school anyway."

So we did. Kenzie even tried some of the spiked punch. Not much. But at least she tried a little. We both grabbed some of the punch and went out back, to a small community park between several of the frat houses. We snagged a couple of swings. No one was around to hear us or bother us.

"You know what I really want?" Kenzie said in between tentative sips of her spiked punch.

I lifted an eyebrow at her. "What?"

"A tattoo!"

"Why don't you get one?" I said, taking much larger sips of the punch. Not exactly Dewar's on ice, but it would have to do.

"My folks would kill me."

At first I laughed out loud, then sobered at the look on her face.

"Okay, I see your point." And I did. I knew my parents would absolutely freak if they knew about the Yamaha, the Crow Bar, the drinking, the smoking. But it really grated on me. I almost told her that she could do what she wanted, that it would be okay. But I didn't. I kept that to myself and just listened.

"But I have done something else," she said mysteriously.

"What?"

"Here, look," she said and folded down the waist on her skirt a little.

I looked down. Kenzie had pierced her belly

button with a tiny gold ring. "Well, what do you know," I said, smiling broadly. "When?"

"This summer, after camp. Holly and I stopped at a little town on the way home. My parents have no idea. They would *die*. Nobody else but Holly knows."

"I do."

"Yeah, well, except you, now."

Kenzie and I looked at each other. It had taken a lot of nerve for her to pierce her belly button and even more nerve to tell someone about it.

Out here, sitting on swings, in the middle of Virginia's campus with no one else around, I felt connected. To Kenzie, to a day when I would finally be on my own. I know Kenzie felt it too. For the first time she could see what it would be like. And I was part of that feeling.

I felt this overwhelming powerful emotion. I wanted to stop the swing, walk over, and kiss her. It startled me, that feeling. I'd come to Virginia just for fun. And then I'd run into a girl like Kenzie. It made me wonder if I could trust her with some of my own dark secrets.

"Kenzie, good for you," I said.

"Yeah, well, I've never done anything like that before."

Kenzie looked over at me again. She had given me something. She trusted me with a secret, something she couldn't tell her own parents about.

And without thinking it through anymore, I took two steps toward her, leaned over, and kissed her. Kenzie didn't pull back.

I'd kissed Sierra plenty since we'd started dating.

But with Sierra it was only a kiss, kind of like trying on expensive clothes. You had to get things just right.

With Kenzie, it was something else. We both had secrets. We both gave a part of each other. The kiss was a way to share. With each other.

But at that moment—to be perfectly honest— I wasn't thinking at all about Sierra. Not at all. There was only Kenzie and me. And we were a long way from Highview.

I'd wanted to call Kenzie at the end of summer. I had picked up the phone about 16 times a day after I'd gotten back from the University of Virginia. I had her number memorized. But I didn't make the call. I couldn't figure out how to make it work.

Don't get me wrong. It wasn't like I cared all that much about Sierra. I didn't. Not really. Oh yeah, I liked her. She was fun to be with, the way she was always making everything seem so special and extraordinary. I liked it when she was around. She was always saying, "Let's make a memory." She made millions of them.

But I could walk away at any time. No problem. Sierra didn't know that, of course. She probably thought I was the one. At least she acted like it when she was around me. When we started school, everyone knew we were together. It just was. Nobody thought otherwise.

There was this part of me, though, this strange part of me, that didn't want to hurt Sierra. I didn't know if it was my conscience or what. I wasn't sure if I had a conscience.

It was simply this feeling that I didn't need to go out of my way to hurt Sierra. That maybe she might be more fragile than she looked. At least I felt a twinge when I thought about it. So I didn't call Kenzie. But I couldn't forget that kiss. Or the connection we'd made. Weird, I know. But it was true. Like we knew more about each other than anyone else knew . . .

I didn't see Kenzie again until the start of school and some crazy toga thing that Sierra really cared about. She'd told me she'd convinced Kenzie, as her new best friend, to dress in a mirror-image toga. I couldn't believe the Kenzie I'd met at Virginia would fall for that. Sierra looked pretty silly. And so did Kenzie. Kenzie and I didn't say a word, but she gave me a little eye roll, as if to say, *Yeah, this toga thing is pretty lame, huh?*

On the second day of school, I passed Kenzie in the hall. "Hey," I said to her. It was strange and awkward.

"Hey," she answered back. I couldn't help but notice how great she looked. Everyone else was noticing too. We eyed each other briefly and kept moving. Neither of us quite knew what to do. I know I sure didn't. She disappeared around the corner, looking for her next class.

"Hey," I said, starting Round Two after our next class.

Kenzie smiled. "Hey, back."

We both stopped this time. I glanced around to see who was watching and listening. Kenzie glanced around as well. It was safe.

"You know, I almost called you every day," I admitted.

"Me too."

"But I didn't."

"I know."

"I should have. Called, I mean."

"I understand. Really. Sierra's great."

It was a stupid conversation. But neither of us knew what to say. What could we say? How could we fix this? How could either of us make this work? We couldn't.

Unless we ignored that part inside that said what we were doing—what we were thinking about, really— was wrong. Looking at Kenzie there in the hall after second period, I knew. I was going to ignore that part and move on.

"Wanna go with me somewhere after school? You'll be surprised. I have an idea," I said suddenly.

"Go with you? Where?"

"Like I said, it's a surprise. So are you in?"

She hesitated for only an instant. "Okay, sure, I'm in."

"We'll take my SUV. Meet me out behind the gym, near the weight room, right after school."

"What about Sierra?"

"Don't worry—she has yearbook committee stuff. We'll be back when it ends."

15

I had no idea where the thought had come from. It appeared from somewhere. And once it had made its appearance, I knew where to go from there.

Kenzie was waiting for me in the doorway when I pulled the Explorer around behind the school. She practically jumped into the Explorer and threw her bag in the back. I pulled out of the parking lot before anyone could see us.

"So where are we going?"

"You'll see," I said mysteriously.

I wasn't entirely sure where the place was, but I had a decent idea. I'd asked a couple of kids, and they'd given me directions. And once we got close, I could always ask around.

But the place was exactly where one of the kids had said it would be. It wasn't in the greatest part of town, but a few kids swore by the place.

When we pulled up in front and parked, Kenzie whispered, "A tattoo parlor! No way! I'm not going to—"

"Don't worry. I am," I interrupted, suddenly very sure of myself, just like I always felt when I kicked the Yamaha into high gear in the middle of the tunnel. I could do what I wanted. Who could tell me I couldn't?

"*You're* getting a tattoo?" Kenzie gasped.

I nodded.

"No way."

"Watch."

"But what will people *say?*" Kenzie asked.

"What do I care? It's not like I'm getting it on my forehead or something."

"Where are you getting one?"

"I don't know." And, honestly, I didn't know. I hadn't exactly thought this through. "I thought I might leave it up to you."

That startled her. "Me?"

I smiled broadly. "Sure, why not? You can choose."

"Oh, my," Kenzie said, her voice barely audible. "Have you thought about what you want?"

I laughed at that one. "No, I haven't. I guess you can choose that too."

Kenzie just stared at me. This was a little more than she was prepared for. I could see that. But I could also see that she liked it, the slight kookiness of it all. And it wasn't like *she* was getting the tattoo. I was. She was only an observer.

"Okay, how about a little soccer ball? It's what

you love. It would mean something." Kenzie's eyes burned brightly. It was clear she was getting into this.

A soccer ball? Okay, sure, I can buy that. It made as much sense as anything else. "Great, a soccer ball. That's gotta be easy. So where?"

Kenzie tilted her head to one side, thinking. "Well . . ."

"I don't want it in some bizarre place, like over my heart. That would be too weird."

Kenzie's face lit up. "How about your ankle? You know, like where you kick the ball when you score? People will see it when you're wearing sandals, but it'll be covered up by socks."

I started to nod. "Okay, yeah, I can do that. My ankle. I don't know anyone who has a soccer ball on their ankle."

"You'll be the first."

"The first. I like that."

We headed into the tattoo parlor. It was pretty disgusting and run-down. Maybe it wasn't such a great idea after all. But the tattoo man was funny, and I liked him. He had me in the chair before I could change my mind, and he had the design in front of me before I could get up and bolt.

Kenzie sat and watched, her part done. I could see she couldn't believe it. But the soccer ball went on my ankle, forever and ever. It was our thing. I'd done it, and there was no taking it back.

It took almost no time at all. I had a small soccer ball tattooed on my ankle. I couldn't tell you why. But it was there. And Kenzie was part of it all.

16

I couldn't beat him. He was this old guy,
way past his prime, and I just couldn't make it work.
I kept trying and trying . . .

"You give it away every time, Ryun," he said.
"Every single time. I know—"

"There's no way," I interrupted, thoroughly
disgusted. "You're lyin'."

Asher James stopped in the middle of the artifi-
cial turf soccer field, planted both feet wide, and put
his hands on his hips. "I'm *what?*"

"You heard me," I muttered, more quietly now.

Asher started laughing. His laugh was infectious.
It was the kind of laugh that made you join in. You
couldn't help yourself. It drew you in, made you
think of everything silly you'd always wanted to do,
be a part of. It made you remember that, really, you

were still a kid and that you could just have fun. You didn't always have to be serious.

"Yeah, I heard you," he said. "And you're a big baby."

"I'm *what?*" I asked, mimicking him.

Asher James, my club coach, was everything my high school soccer coach was not. Frank Jenkins ran his high school team with an iron fist, knew nothing about soccer, liked to scream a lot, and told anyone who asked how great a coach he was because I'd helped his team be a winner the past two years.

Asher was none of those. He'd been my club coach since I was 10. There was no messin' around with Asher. He knew his stuff. He'd been a major player in his day. He'd been all-ACC and an all-American one year at Clemson. He'd been to the Final Four twice in college.

I'd looked him up on the Internet and seen for myself that he'd been quite a defender in his day. He was the marking back the Clemson coach always relied on to take the other team's best striker completely out of the game.

For three straight years, as Clemson made its run at a national championship, Asher was the guy they always mentioned as the anchor on defense.

"I tore my ACL in my senior year at Clemson," Asher told me once.

"Partial or whole tear?"

"All the way through," Asher had said. "I was sure my life was over. I rehabbed every day for a year and a half, but I was never really the same again."

It was a nasty tear, Asher had said. A big kid on Wake Forest had come after him, cleats up, on a cold fall afternoon. Asher was facing sideways to the kid. The cleats had gone right through the side of his left knee, shredding the tendons and ligaments. There was almost no way to repair it. They tried. But it didn't work very well.

"I tried to come back," Asher had told me. "I ran a million miles. I climbed a thousand hills. I ran hundreds of stadium stairs."

Asher had tried two A League teams—one step below the highest professional league in the country.

"But I couldn't make it," he told me. "I was a step too slow. You don't come back from that kind of injury. It isn't possible, not without a miracle of some sort."

Asher believed in miracles. I didn't. I was harsh. I thought life was exactly what you had in front of you. But not Asher. He believed in a God who would, to use his words, "patiently grant you the wisdom to understand pain and suffering that came your way without rhyme or reason." He believed in a God who would help him through the trouble, get to the other side.

I thought Asher was crazy. I saw no God, no understanding. Only a tough break—some kid on an opposing team had mangled him. And where was the justice? Where was the part of that event that made sense? It didn't. But Asher thought it did.

He believed there was a reason for everything. He believed—he really did believe, because he brought it up often—that God honored your commitment and effort, that there was a reason for any pain—even the kind that alters your life forever.

"It's all good," he told me. "All good."

"Yeah, right," I'd fired back at him. "Show me. Tell me. How is this good?"

How does it make sense that some mindless senseless injury would end everything you'd worked for your entire life? How does that fit into some plan that a God you can't see might have for you?

"Maybe it meant that I would wind up as your coach," he'd said. "If I was playing, I wouldn't be your coach. And if I wasn't your coach, then where would *you* be?"

"I'd be torching you on the field in the MLS one day," I'd laughed right back at him. "You'd be trying to mark me in your sorry way, and I'd take you every time. I'd spin you like a top and cost you your job. You'd be watching me put it in the back of the net."

It wasn't true, of course. I could only imagine what it would be like to try to score on someone like Asher when he was healthy and in his prime. It would be a nightmare. He must have been a beast in his day. But I would never tell him that.

And, in my heart, I knew there was something to what Asher said. If he hadn't had his knee ripped apart, then he wouldn't have been forced to the sideline and into coaching. I wouldn't have met him when I was 10, he wouldn't have worked with me almost every day for seven years, and he wouldn't have turned me into the soccer player I was right now.

I had the speed and size to be a really good player. Without a coach like Asher I probably would have been a really good player. But Asher was an amazing coach, like none I'd ever seen in youth soccer. He'd made me a *great* striker, not just a good one. I would never, ever tell him this, but I knew that I could now go to any college in the country because of Asher. He'd taught me every conceivable way to beat any defense, in any given situation or formation.

For seven years, he'd taught me how to score and move from any place on a soccer field. He'd taught me courage, how not to fear anything in my path, how to be selfish with the ball when necessary but how to work with others when necessary too.

I was Asher's guy. And if he had not been there when I arrived, then it was true, I would be a different person. Asher's exit as a soccer player and entry as my coach had changed the order of things. But that didn't mean I believed in his God.

I had already played three times with the national youth team in three international tournaments. I'd scored 11 goals in nine games on those trips. I had discovered that kids were the same around the world as they were in my own country. They couldn't stop me in South Korea, Japan, Brazil, or Ghana. I could score on those kids as well.

But first there had been Asher. He was the first to show me how to go forward in life without worrying about what might happen. Day after long day, he'd worked with me until I was so comfortable with a soccer ball at my feet and a plan in front of me that

I felt like I knew what to do in every conceivable situation.

But the fact that he'd been with me every day as my coach—not waiting to mark me on some professional soccer field when I finally made my debut there some day—didn't mean I fell for everything he believed in. Like his God. There was no plan there. It was total dumb, stupid, bad luck on Asher's part. And truly nice fortune on mine.

"A big baby, who still gives himself away every time," Asher said today, now. He was always pushing, always testing, making sure I never got too comfortable in my skin.

"How? What are you talking about?" I asked him.

Asher pulled the soccer ball back, away from me. He tapped it a couple of times with his right foot. "How many times have we talked about what a top defender looks for?"

I looked down. Only about 10 million times. "The socks and the ball."

"And no top defender cares about your good looks or your cute smile or your hips or your rear that the girls admire. Right?"

"Right," I said, laughing. "They watch my socks to see where I'm moving the ball. It's the ball they key on. That's what they have to take from me."

"Before your speed takes them, yes." Asher gathered the ball at his feet and took a step toward me. "And do you know what you always do, when you really, really want to beat someone? Like you do me, right now?"

"What?"

"Your plant foot."

"My what?"

"The foot that you move out forward prominently on whatever move you're making. That's how I know which way you're going."

I stared at him in shock. "No way! I don't do that—"

"Yes, you do. You don't do it when you're playing, but you do it with me, because you're thinking you need that extra jump on me, that extra half step to get around me. So it doesn't hurt you right now. But it will some day, against a really good defender at the top level."

Asher turned his back to me, shielding. "Here, watch. You do it this way, even when you're posting up on me." He moved with his back toward me, until we made contact. I pushed back with my hands but watched his feet and the ball. "When you're getting ready to make a move on me, you do this."

He took one step toward his left with his left foot, planting it slightly behind him as he got ready to make his move. The ball was still back, but I could see what he was talking about. I could see that he was going to his left—my left too—even though the ball hadn't moved yet. When he made his move, I reached through his legs—knowing which direction the ball would be going—and flicked the ball away.

He did it again, this time making the first plant move with his right foot and leaning into me a little. It made no difference where the ball was. I knew where he was going and flicked the ball away again.

Then he turned and played, facing me. When he

planted his right foot, I anticipated that direction—
even though the ball was on his left foot—and
flicked it away again as he tried to cross over and
move it to the foot that was already a half step to
my side. I could see it. It was like he was trying to
cheat, get that extra half step before he'd actually
made a move.

"See?"

"Yeah, I see," I said grudgingly.

"It's the same with a move as it is with a shot.
Just as you never let a keeper know which foot
you're going to use, which direction you're going
to shoot, until the last possible moment, it's the
same with a defender. Don't give away your direction until you have to, not even against the fastest
defender in the world."

"I didn't think I was doing that."

"You don't, usually. But against me, when every
half step matters, you do."

"So what do I do about it?"

"In games, for the first few times you go up
against a marking back, it's like poker. Bluff a few
times, even if you fail. Lose the ball to the marking
back in weird ways, unpredictable ways. Don't let
him see a pattern. Then, when you need to beat
him to score, he can't anticipate. Plant foot forward,
backward, sideways. It doesn't matter. He won't
know which way you might or might not go. Make
sense?"

I nodded. It did make sense. It almost always did
with Asher. He had this ability to get right at it, break
it down so I could see it and grasp it intuitively.

We'd been at it, one-on-one, for nearly an hour. Both of our shirts were soaked through with sweat. The rest of my team was just starting to show up, and I'd already gotten a full workout in. It had been that way with us for several years. Asher had been my mentor and tutor like this since I'd hit puberty.

"Okay, we're done," he said. "Work on it in practice today?"

"Got it," I said, and turned to jog over and join my team.

"Hey!" he called out to me. "So where are you? Have you decided on Duke?"

I turned, squared both feet, and then took an exaggerated step backward with one of them. "Don't know," I said loudly. "We'll see which way I go."

Asher smiled. "Good boy."

17

I'm not sure how Kenzie found out. But I'm glad she knew. It made it easier somehow.

She told me casually on a Wednesday night. We were sitting out back on her porch. She was playing the guitar for me. Her parents, sister, Lark, and the twins were at church. I'd lied to Sierra again about where I was. I didn't feel guilty about it. Kenzie did.

"You know, it's all right," Kenzie said in a quiet voice.

"What?"

"That you do . . . things you're not supposed to."

I stared hard at Kenzie. "Like . . . ?"

Kenzie didn't look away. "Like smoking. I found them. The cigarettes you keep in the back."

I blinked several times. "You did? How?"

Kenzie smiled. "By accident, when I put my

sweater back there before a football game. But, Ryun, I knew already . . ."

"Yeah?"

"Yeah, I did. I can usually figure things out."

"Hmm," I said. "So what else do you know?"

"Well, there is one thing," she said slowly. "I was kind of curious about the helmet you left in your SUV twice. Where'd it come from?"

Wow. Kenzie was sharp. I'd left my motorcycle helmet in the Explorer by accident just twice—and Kenzie had spotted it both times. She didn't miss anything.

"You really wanna know?"

Kenzie nodded. She began to put the guitar away in its case. "Yes, I do."

I got up to leave. Kenzie followed. We didn't say a word as we got in my Explorer. Kenzie didn't ask where we were going.

When we got to the pipe and I pulled the tarp off the Yamaha, I handed the helmet to Kenzie. "Here, you can wear this," I said. "The strap is really easy. Just pull it tight."

Kenzie pulled the helmet on and tucked her hair in. I could see that she was scared. Her legs were wobbly, and her hands trembled as she tried to pull the straps tight.

"Don't worry," I said, taking one of her hands. "I'll go slow, and I'll be careful."

"I've never done anything like this before," she said, the fear showing in her voice.

"It'll be fine," I reassured her. "You'll like it. Just hold on to me."

I fired up the Yamaha. I would take her through the pipe first. But very slowly. The dark alone would probably freak her out, but she'd be okay. I felt sure Kenzie could handle it.

Kenzie had a death grip around my waist as we got started. But that was fine with me. I didn't mind.

As we entered the pipe, a soft moan escaped from Kenzie. But she recovered quickly and just held on tighter. I glanced around. She was staring ahead bravely. Well, good for her.

To Kenzie, the trip through that pipe was almost certainly unlike anything she'd ever experienced. It was tame to me, because I was going only about 30 mph, but it must have seemed like the speed of light to Kenzie.

When we roared out the other end, Kenzie squeezed hard, once. "That was cool!" she yelled, her voice muffled some from the helmet faceplate.

"I know," I called back. "It's a rush."

I turned and headed out to the streets. I took the routes I knew well, the ones I always raced along when I wanted to clear my head. But I went slowly, deliberately. I didn't want to frighten Kenzie. I just wanted her to get a sense of what it was all like. Even so, I could feel every part of Kenzie's body trembling as she held on to me for dear life.

When we finally got back to the pipe, I put the bike in park. Kenzie pulled the helmet free when she could get her strength back again and dropped it beside the motorcycle. I pulled one leg over and then reversed my position on the motorcycle so I was facing her. I took her in my arms and kissed her. Kenzie

ryun's story

119

responded eagerly, still weak from the trip, then collapsed into my arms. I held her silently for a very long time.

Then I held her tightly as we kissed. It lasted for a very long time. I had never shared my Yamaha with anyone before—not until Kenzie. And I think she knew that. I had given her part of my secret world. And there was no changing that.

As I pulled up in front of Sierra's house at 7:30 in the morning, I switched over the FM stations in my Explorer and popped a breath mint. I'd already had my morning cigarette, and the pack was safely tucked away in the spare wheel compartment.

I had a system now. It had gotten really old switching all the presets on the radio every time I picked Sierra up. So I'd taken a risk and made the FM2 stations mine and the FM1 stations Sierra's.

I knew Sierra would never figure out that the first six stations—the ones she always switched back and forth when we drove together—were hers and that the next six were mine.

It was a little like the double life I was leading. I always had to keep the Sierra and Kenzie things separate, even when we were all together. I had to make sure things I knew about Kenzie that she'd never shared with anyone didn't leak into conversations with Sierra. Actually, I liked it. Trying to keep everything straight between Sierra and Kenzie, I mean.

When I was in Sierra's world, it was all yearbook pictures, cool clothes, expensive shoes, holding hands, and making memories. When I was with Kenzie, it was just us, because we didn't dare go out in public.

It had gotten especially hard in the last few weeks. Kenzie and Sierra were becoming inseparable best friends. It was really annoying. I could never quite figure out who Kenzie was most interested in hanging with—Sierra or me. Kenzie and I had this soul connection. But I could also tell that Kenzie was fascinated with Sierra and being a part of her world, the elite crowd.

I found out things about Kenzie that she never told anyone. I especially liked our Wednesdays together—just sitting in her room or out back on the porch, listening to her play her silly songs on the guitar. She would never play them for anyone else at Highview. That would be too embarrassing. But she played them for me. That was one of the things that hooked me—I liked the fact she trusted me that much.

I suspect school had always been the best thing going for Sierra. She'd been popular since the dawn of time. Kenzie was only starting to figure it out. So it was strange going back and forth between the two of them. Their worlds had always been separate.

Until now. Not only was I part of both worlds, but Kenzie had become a permanent bright moon in orbit around the Sierra sun. Holly had brought her in, Sierra had fully accepted her, and Kenzie was thrilled to be part of it all.

Sometimes Kenzie couldn't help herself. We'd be talking, and she'd go on and on about Sierra. She adored Sierra. It almost made her forget that she was going behind her new "best friend's" back and stealing her boyfriend away from her.

I took Sierra to and from school every day. It was a royal pain for me, because I had to get up half an hour earlier than I would otherwise in order to get from my crummy neighborhood to hers. But I knew Sierra liked it. So it wasn't like I had a choice. And it was a small price to pay, really, for being a part of Sierra's world.

So every morning I left the Explorer running and walked up the driveway to their house. I didn't have to. Sierra would have been happy to meet me at the SUV every morning. But it gave me a chance each day to further snow Sierra's mom, now very much on my side.

I was sure that every boy Sierra had dated had avoided her parents like the plague. Not me. I liked the challenge of sparring with her mom. It was fun.

"Good morning, Mrs. Reynolds. How are you today?" I asked when she opened the door even before I'd had a chance to ring the doorbell.

"Come in, Ryun," Mrs. Reynolds said. "Have you had breakfast? Would you like anything?"

I smiled. She asked me every morning. "No,

thank you, Mrs. Reynolds. I'm good," I answered, just as I had every morning since the start of school.

"Okay, then. Sierra will be down shortly, I'm sure."

I liked Sierra's mom. She was an adult version of Sierra—the perfect figure, perfect hair, perfect clothes . . . From watching her mom, I had a pretty good idea what Sierra would be like as an adult.

"Hey!" Sierra called out from the top of the stairs. I glanced up, startled as always whenever I saw her. I swear Sierra had 365 separate sets of clothes for every day of the year and even more pairs of shoes. Maybe more than that, because she changed clothes again at the end of the day before we went out.

I didn't mind. I liked that about girls, that they paid so much attention to stuff like that. I liked that they were meticulous about what they did with their eyes, their lips, their fingernails, their toes, and every other part of their body. There was something amazing about it all. Like temple worship. That's the way I always looked at it.

"Hey, back," I answered softly.

She bounded down the stairs and linked arms with me, guiding me from the house. Her hand slid easily into mine. It was nice, comfortable. I felt a twinge of guilt as I compared that slender hand to Kenzie's, which also slid easily into mine. But it passed quickly. I didn't believe in guilt. I only believed in what worked or didn't. And right now, I was dating two incredible girls—and getting away with it.

She tucked her head into my shoulder as we walked down the sidewalk. "You know, I don't have yearbook today. . . ."

"Why not? What gives?"

"Two of the girls have doctors' appointments, so they canceled."

"Mm-hmm."

"So can we do something? After school?"

I squeezed her hand. I knew what she wanted. Window-shopping for shoes at the mall. I now knew that this was, without a doubt, her favorite thing in the world. Sierra was most happy when she had her nose pressed up against the glass, looking down at a pair of $500 shoes.

So I'd gotten in the habit of spotting the most expensive shoe stores I could find, anywhere. And I'd found this amazing place at a new premium out-let mall someone had just started at the other end of town. I was sure they had the most expensive shoes on the planet. Maybe even a pair of shoes that cost more than $1,000. Sierra would be thrilled.

"I was thinking maybe we could go to that new outlet mall," I answered.

Sierra looked up at me, wide-eyed. "Really? Can we go?"

"Absolutely. Your wish is my command."

It was such a small price to pay for happiness. It certainly didn't hurt me. It wasn't like I had to pay for the shoes, just everything else on the excursion. But the shoes weren't part of the deal, thank goodness.

"Also . . ."

"Yes?" I knew that tone of voice. Sierra wanted something else.

"You know homecoming is coming up this

Friday, and Holly's organizing a party at her house afterwards. We can go, right? Even if you have a game on Saturday?"

I did have a soccer game on Saturday, and staying out late the night before a game was a lousy idea. But I could manage. I always did. "Sure, no problem. My game's later," I lied. "I can sleep in."

Sierra squeezed my hand. Simple joys and simple pleasures. It sure was nice to be in Sierra's world.

Kenzie was so sad. But there was nothing
I could do about it. Not on such a night.

We all sat together at the football game—Sierra,
Kenzie, me, our friends. It killed Kenzie at things like
this, because Sierra would stay so close to me, while
she was forced to hang out nearby. Away from me.

Our football team was terrible. But no one cared.
No one actually watched the game. That wasn't the
point. It was only a chance to run around a little,
yell, walk back and forth from the restroom to the
stands, and hang out. And party, of course. There
was always that.

I think our team won. I'm not sure. I think we
ran the ball from inside the 20-yard line in the fourth
quarter and scored. Then again, I wasn't paying any
attention. So I could be wrong. I don't know.

I *do* know that everyone was in a good mood at Holly's after-party, though. So we must have won the game. The football team was really drunk, so I guess we did win.

It took all kinds of restraint not to have a few myself. But I was a big-time athlete. I didn't drink. Everyone knew that. Sierra, Kenzie, and I were always the designated drivers.

But I was wired after I dropped Sierra off at her house. Totally wired. So I drove over to the Crow Bar and had a couple. Maybe three. And then, for fun, I drove over to the pipe and my Yamaha. I wasn't ready for the night to end.

I pulled the tarp off the Yamaha and fired her up. No pipe tonight. I wanted a little action, so I wheeled her around and headed off for the city.

It felt good to get out. I liked the feel of the bike. I liked weaving in and out of traffic, unbound by the lanes that held cars to one side or another.

I was free to do and go as I pleased. I could ignore the usual rules. There were very few cars around, and the lights didn't seem to hold my attention.

After I'd stopped briefly at a light, a cop pulled up beside me rather casually, rolled his window down, and pointed at me. No lights flashing. Just a very serious man in an unmarked car. He motioned for me to pull the bike over.

I almost made a run for it. Almost. My adrenaline surged like you wouldn't believe. I knew I was still slightly drunk, probably over the legal limit. I glanced over at the side of the road. If I jumped the curb, I could disappear in a heartbeat. His car couldn't follow my bike.

"Don't do it, son," the cop said just loud enough for me to hear over the noise from my bike's engine. "I got your license plate, and I'll find you. Park it."

I closed my eyes. The world was spinning a little. I was in for it now. There wasn't much I could do. If I ran, he'd find me. And I'd be in a whole lot more trouble for running away from a cop. So I parked it.

I knew then that he'd watched me weave through traffic, through red lights, occasionally speeding. There was no saving grace. I'd hoped— almost prayed—that the cold night air and the ride had given me enough time to sober up to the legal limit. No chance.

I failed the breath test. Drunk driving and reckless driving. I'd lose my license for sure.

So just like that, I was caught. No flashing lights and big fireworks—only a guy in an unmarked car watching me tool around. No grinding metal car chases. At least that would have been exciting. It was just this middle-aged guy with almost no hair observing me in my natural habitat.

I called Asher from the police station. He came over right away. He didn't say anything to me when he came into the station. He spoke quietly to the police, away from me, for a long time. He glanced over at me a couple of times. He shook hands with them and then took me with him.

I felt naked, like I'd been stripped and left to die on the side of the road. I didn't know what to think, what I was doing, what it all meant. Getting caught had slipped up on me so quickly.

"You know you're in a lot of trouble, right?" Asher said on the ride to my house.

"Yeah, I know."

"It's bad. You'll have to go to court. You'll almost certainly lose your license."

"Yeah, I know."

"And I don't have to tell you how stupid this is, what it might mean to a scholarship?"

"Yeah, I know."

Asher didn't say anything for a long time. He let me stew. I was grateful. I didn't feel like talking.

"Okay," he said finally. "I'll help. I have a friend, a lawyer, who's good at this sort of thing. He can probably get you probation. You won't go to juvenile detention or anything. He'll clean it up as much as possible."

"Thanks," I mumbled.

"And I'll make sure it doesn't hurt you with schools," Asher continued. "But you know you'll have to deal with your parents, right? You do know that?"

"Yeah, I know," I said miserably. But a plan was already hatching. I might be able to get out of this. With a little luck. "I'll talk to them about all of this."

"Promise?"

"Yeah, I promise," I lied.

"Okay, but one more of these and you're done. Understand? One more stunt like this and you're finished."

"Okay."

"I mean it, Ryun. All of it has to stop. Drinking. Smoking. Running around. It all has to stop."

I was so miserable, I didn't even think to wonder how Asher knew about any of this . . . until later. "It will," I promised.

Asher glanced over at me to make sure I got it. I nodded. I got it. But I also felt like a man pulled back from the gallows. I'd survived the hanging. It would be okay. I could still bluff my way through all of this. I would make it through this night, as bad as it was. Not exactly unscathed. But not maimed and left to die on the side of the street. There was that. It was something, at least.

It was the dumbest thing.

I could never quite figure out why Kenzie had a boyfriend. She didn't even like the guy. Taylor Hatfield was a football jock, a loser without a future. And he didn't have the best reputation with girls either. But I guess Kenzie had to have someone. Because she sure wasn't going to tell anyone about *us*.

Still, it always bugged me to see the two of them together. I really hated it when he put his arm around her and drew her face close to his. I only wanted *my* face that close to Kenzie's.

Yeah, so I'm a big fat hypocrite. I knew it killed Kenzie to see Sierra and me together. So I shouldn't have minded that Kenzie had a boyfriend. But I did mind. It bothered me—a lot.

What Kenzie and I had together was something

very different than what Sierra and I had. Did I love Kenzie? I wasn't sure. But it was something stronger than I had with Sierra.

So I can't say I was upset when Kenzie finally had the sense to break up with the loser the week before our last football game. *Great. See ya. Go hide under a rock somewhere,* I thought, when I first found out about it from Sierra.

Kenzie made a big deal about it with Sierra, Holly, and Carin. A lot of crying, girl stuff. I ignored all of it. Sierra thought it was terrible that a guy would break up before the last game of the year. I don't think she had a clue that Kenzie was the one who'd ended it. Funny how girls are about that. I knew it was mostly an act by Kenzie. She didn't care at all for the guy, so it was high time she got rid of him. She cared for me.

Kenzie and I had been really careful. We had Wednesdays to ourselves, but I left before her family got home from church. And whenever we could, when Sierra was busy, we spent time together at places where no one in Sierra's crowd would go. Like this cool park, where we'd walk and see only old people.

Still, I think Holly knew about us. Or at least she guessed. But I was pretty sure no one else did. It was our private thing, something we kept all to ourselves. And I liked it that way.

I know Kenzie had thought about telling Sierra. She'd probably been close more than once. It wasn't in Kenzie's nature to keep things secret like this for so long. She was so open, so honest, so trustworthy.

It wasn't easy for her, like it was for me. I'd kept
secrets for so long that to me, I really did live two
separate lives. And I was comfortable with that.

But I still wasn't sure how I felt about Kenzie
telling Sierra. Part of me didn't care all that much.
Sierra had had lots of boyfriends. I knew she'd get
over it. I still liked Sierra, but some of the glow of
being in her circle was wearing off. I knew for sure
that I wasn't in love with her.

But Kenzie? She was someone I could talk to.
So if I had to choose, I'd probably choose Kenzie.
But it wasn't some big thing. If Kenzie should tell
Sierra about us, well, then I'd deal with it. Why
bother unless it really was a problem?

Since homecoming, I'd been distracted. Thank
heavens for Kenzie. She kept me sane. She was the
only one I dared tell about what happened and that
I was going to lose my license. I knew she would
help me any way I asked and keep it all between
the two of us.

Asher had gotten a lawyer. But I'd continued
my lie with Asher. I told him that I'd spoken to my
parents and that I'd been grounded for eternity.
But, in fact, I had never told my parents.

It had worked like a charm. On the day of the
court date, I had called Asher frantically and told
him that my dad couldn't go with me and my mom
couldn't speak English well enough. Asher had agreed
to stand in as my guardian rather than postpone the
court date.

Asher had been right. I lost my license. But it
wasn't too bad. No one knew at school, so I kept

driving. I hid my Explorer well away from the soccer
practice field so Asher couldn't tell how I'd gotten
there. When he asked once, I told him I was catching
a ride there with others on the team, which happened a lot. Everybody caught rides with everyone
else all the time. It wasn't a big deal.

I wasn't going to get caught again. No way. I
could handle it now. I'd just be more careful. I'd be
smart about it.

■ ■ ■

The week before the last game, Kenzie had been
revved up.

"I can't take this anymore," she'd told me that
Wednesday night when we were together, sitting
on her parents' couch. She had been strumming
her guitar when she stopped suddenly and turned
to me. "I want to tell Sierra everything."

I hadn't known what to say. I'd grown tired
of the Sierra-Kenzie game. But I wasn't sure how
to end anything or which way to go.

"Fine, tell her," I'd said.

Kenzie had started to cry. "But Sierra is so nice.
I can't do this to her now. I can't. But I'm so con-
fused—when I'm with you, when I'm with Taylor.
And then when I'm with Sierra."

"So make it simple," I'd answered. "Break up
with Taylor. You don't even like him all that much.
Then you only have to deal with Sierra and me."

Kenzie had kept crying. But I knew what she was
thinking. I knew her that well now.

So it was no shock at all when she broke up with Taylor later that week.

But what I didn't know—what I couldn't figure—was what would come next. Would Kenzie tell Sierra? Would she give up Sierra's world to be with me? Would Sierra ever forgive me for going behind her back? Did I care? Or would we keep on doing what we were doing now?

It was the last football game of our
senior year, and, as usual, Sierra was making a
major deal over it. We had to do something special.
We had to "make a memory."

So she convinced her dad to give her his classic
'57 Chevy for the game. She picked Kenzie up, then
me. All the two of them talked about on the drive
over to the football game was Kenzie and Taylor's
breakup. I didn't say anything for the entire drive
to the football game. Sierra was so understanding
with Kenzie. I wondered what Kenzie was up to—
she had a determined look on her face. Was tonight
the night she'd have enough guts to tell Sierra
about us?

I stashed a couple of cigarettes in my pocket, in
the tin case with my breath mints. By halftime, I'd

excused myself twice to smoke them out behind the stadium, among the trees, where nobody would see me. I was getting nervous. I had this feeling. Kenzie was acting so strange. She and Holly kept disappearing. I knew they had to be talking, plotting.

And then, after Sierra got back from a trip to the john, she got a little spooky too. She wasn't her usual "make a memory" cheery self. She didn't even smile when I handed her a Coke, and she didn't say anything the rest of the game.

Our very own Highview Hornets football team won its final game. I paid no attention. I just wanted to get away, go drive somewhere.

"Let's get pizza," I said when the game ended.

"Great," Kenzie said. Her voice had an edge to it. She'd decided something.

I glanced over at Sierra. She was glaring hard at Kenzie. There was such malice in those eyes, it was a little scary. I'd never seen Sierra like this, not ever. Something was going on, something I didn't quite get. And which, I was certain, I didn't have a whole lot of control over. I'd learned you didn't get in the middle of catfights, ever.

"Fine," Sierra said curtly.

Kenzie turned to Holly, Carin, and the others. "Are you guys . . . ?"

"No!" Sierra said sharply. "Just us. Let's go." She turned, leaving me in the dust, and walked away.

I trailed behind. I cast a sidelong glance at Kenzie. "What gives?" I whispered.

"Don't know," she whispered back.

We marched through the parking lot outside the

football stadium. Sierra was up to something. She was walking by herself, which never happened. She got to the '57 Chevy long before either of us did. She climbed in the car and waited.

I opened the passenger side of the car and slid in beside Sierra. Kenzie got in and closed the passenger-side door. Sierra gunned the engine, not bothering to put on her seat belt, and floored it. She almost hit a light pole on the way out of the parking lot.

"Sierra, slow down!" I said loudly over the roar of the Chevy's engine. What was up with her?

Sierra didn't answer. She pulled the wheel hard to the right, coming out of the parking lot. The tires complained as we made the turn. She didn't let up on the gas as we hit the road. We were already 20 miles an hour over the speed limit by the time we hit Route 58, on our way to the pizza shop we always visited.

"Sierra, please," Kenzie tried. "What's wrong? Why are you so mad?"

Kenzie reached across me, trying to touch Sierra's shoulder. Sierra reacted violently, pulling away from Kenzie. It made the car rock and jump a little as her reaction spilled over onto the steering wheel.

"Don't touch me," Sierra said. Sierra had separated from me as well. I looked at her. She was fighting back tears. Even in the dim light of the car and the road, I could see that her eyes were getting red. She was going to lose it.

"Hey, what gives?" I tried.

Sierra bit her lip hard. She gripped the steering wheel even harder and stepped on the gas. The car jumped forward. I glanced at the speedometer. We were at 75 and still going faster. Something had happened. I'd never seen Sierra so upset. It just wasn't like her.

"Kenzie, how could you?" Sierra finally managed, a couple of tears trickling down one cheek. "How *could* you? You're my best friend. I trusted you with everything . . ." The Chevy sped up again.

I looked over at Kenzie. There was shock first and then a huge wave of relief on her face. So, somehow, Sierra knew about Kenzie and me. That had to be it.

"Sierra, it wasn't like that," Kenzie said quickly.

"Then how was it?" Sierra hissed, her teeth clenched.

"I've wanted to tell you about it for so long." Kenzie's words came out in a rush. She clearly wanted to get this out fast, before it could hurt anymore.

"But you didn't," Sierra said bitterly.

"I desperately wanted to," Kenzie tried to explain. "Ryun and I met at the University of Virginia back at the end of the summer, even before I knew you very well. We talked for a really long time. It just happened. We didn't mean for it to. We got to know each other so fast, we just connected."

Sierra sped up even faster. "You *connected!*" she said, almost shouting. "Who cares about that? Who cares that you talked? Kenzie, you're my best friend! How could you have done this to me?"

I felt trapped. Sierra and Kenzie were going to

kill each other for sure. Maybe even before Sierra killed us with her driving. And I wasn't sure I knew exactly what was going on here. "Sierra," I said soothingly, "are you sure you . . . ?"

"I heard her," Sierra snapped at me. "In the john, talking to Holly. I know. I heard. You two have been going behind my back. I know." The tears really started to come then. She was about to lose control of the car. It was careening wildly from side to side.

"Sierra, come on," I said again. "Please slow down!"

She just glared at me.

Then, at the very moment when I was certain we'd all go right over the edge of the road and slide through the gravel down the slight ditch on the side of the road, Sierra started to slow down. I could see that reality was finally hitting her. She knew now. She knew that it had all been one big lie for her. To her. Her best friend and her boyfriend—the two people she cared about more than all the world—had betrayed her.

She slowed almost to a crawl and then partly pulled off to the side of the road. She couldn't even manage to get the Chevy all the way off. She yanked open the car door and got out. I slid out quickly and followed her. The Chevy was still running.

A car following close behind almost clipped the Chevy as it came upon us, but Sierra didn't care. She headed toward the woods on the other side of the car. Sobbing, irrational, she was completely over the edge. I'd seen her cry only once

before, and it wasn't anything like this. I didn't
know what to do.

"We didn't mean to," I called out to her. "We
didn't mean to. It just happened."

Sierra wheeled around and faced me. The tears
had formed two long streaks of mascara on her face.
She was beside herself. "Just happened!" she yelled
at me. "Kenzie's my best friend."

"I didn't know," I said lamely. "When we got
together in Virginia, I didn't know the two of you
were becoming such good friends. I didn't know."

"Yeah, but you do now," she said, the tears coming again. "You've known all school year." She
started crying hysterically. "And . . . and you *lied*
to me, both of you. You lied." She buried her face
in her hands.

Two more cars raced by, horns blaring. We had
to move the Chevy, with its rear end sticking out
into the highway. Kenzie was still sitting in the car,
but I knew she was too freaked out to think of it.
"Sierra, we've got to move your dad's car. We're
going to cause an accident."

Sierra didn't say anything. I started to walk
toward her, to console her. But she took two steps
away from me. She wanted nothing to do with me.

"Okay," I said calmly. "But I'm moving the car.
Come on. We'll talk it out in the car."

Sierra didn't move, so I went back to the car. I
got in on the driver's side. Kenzie gave me a worried
look, then propped the door open on the passenger
side. I pulled the Chevy completely off to the side of
the road. Then we waited.

After a couple of minutes, Sierra trudged over
to the car and slid in. None of us said anything.
I eased the car back onto the highway. I just started
driving, even though I wasn't sure anymore where
we were going. I picked up speed in silence. I didn't
know what to do or say. So I just gunned the engine
to full speed and drove.

Sierra was crying softly now, her head tucked
against the armrest on the car. She was clearly in
pain. She felt a million miles away.

"I'm *sorry*," Kenzie tried again. "I never meant
for this to happen . . ."

"*Sorry?* That's all you can say? You guys are total
traitors. Liars! I hate you both!" Sierra screamed.
And she started to cry again.

Then, without warning, she reached toward the
car door handle and yanked it. In a flash I could see
that she was about to fling the door open. We were
going at least 60, and she was trying to get out of
the car!

"No!" Kenzie screamed.

I reached across to stop Sierra, but I was too late.
The passenger-side door started to open, the speed
of the car ripping it open.

It all happened at once. The right side of the car
slipped off the side of the road. The rear of the car
started to fishtail. I jerked the car hard to the right,
to keep the door on Sierra's side from ripping open
and tossing her from the car. The Chevy pulled hard
to the right.

And then I lost control as I overcorrected the
other way. The Chevy took one long shuddering

roll sideways on the gravel and then, in a sickening thud, lurched and flipped into the air, upside down. Kenzie and Sierra both screamed. I was powerless to do anything. The car hit, landed, rolled, and smashed, over and over. We were all tossed inside like crash-test dummies.

I felt the rip in my right leg. But it was a distant thing, almost removed from me. Everything around me was a big, careening, smashing blur.

The car finally landed upside down. The dashboard had caved in on us. The car was crumpled, but my door was propped open. The engine was still running. I could see gasoline starting to pour out on the ground. I started to panic at the sight.

I dragged myself out and pulled Kenzie out with me. I couldn't move my right leg. I'd ripped something badly, I knew it.

"Sierra. We have to get Sierra," Kenzie said hoarsely. "She's still inside."

There was a muffled explosion from inside the Chevy's crumpled frame. Something had caught fire. The Chevy was starting to be engulfed in flames. I knew the car would blow, and time was running out.

I took a step toward the other side of the car, where Sierra was still pinned inside, but the pain made me scream. Kenzie was by my side in an instant, helping me walk. I leaned hard on her. We made our way to the other side of the car as quickly as we could.

Sierra was unconscious. Kenzie and I both reached her just as flames started to leap out of the engine. The smoke was everywhere.

"Hurry! I think it's going to blow up!" Kenzie cried.

Sierra wouldn't move. She was totally blacked out. She was also partly stuck in the car. We both pulled as hard as we could until Sierra's limp body finally came free. We dragged her across the ground to a spot about 30 feet from the car.

Then Kenzie and I collapsed in a heap on the ground. Pain was shooting from my right knee. It felt like it had been pulled apart in a million directions.

An instant later the Chevy collapsed in a screaming, dying fit of grinding metal, flames, and billowing smoke. We had barely made it out in time.

When we checked Sierra, we saw that the side of her head was bleeding like crazy. She was still unconscious. We didn't dare move her. Kenzie tried talking to her. She even draped her jacket over Sierra to keep her warm. But Sierra wouldn't wake up. She lay there, not moving. We didn't know what to think. We just didn't know.

22

It wasn't right.

We were heroes, Kenzie and me. For pulling
Sierra from the burning '57 Chevy before it was
completely consumed from the flames. We were on
the front page of the newspaper, all over the local
news. Pictures of Kenzie and me everywhere.

But Sierra wasn't awake yet, and Dr. Snyder
said she might never wake up. She was in a coma.
She just lay there in the bed at University Hospital,
not moving. Not seeing. Not doing anything at all.

When the police and fire engines and ambulances
and the whole rest of the world showed up at the
crash, they all assumed that Sierra had been driving
the car. After all, it was her dad's car. They just
assumed it. Kenzie didn't say anything. I didn't say

anything. So that was the story, and we didn't say anything to contradict it.

Kenzie knew that I'd lost my license. I'd told her, because I knew I could trust her. And Kenzie knew that, if they found out I'd been driving, it would be bad. Really bad. I might be expelled from school, lose my scholarship. Everything.

So when I let the police believe that it was Sierra who'd been driving and didn't correct them, Kenzie let it go too. I figured I could always straighten it out later. But at least I'd have a couple of days to figure it out, maybe talk to Asher about it.

But then they said Sierra might not come out of her coma. They didn't know. So I didn't say anything. I had my own troubles anyway. Losing my license wasn't even at the top of my list.

The force of the crash had partially torn my ACL, as if a defender had come in, cleats up, and caved in the side of my leg. My leg was shredded. They stabilized it with this black temporary brace while I waited for the swelling to go down so I could have surgery.

No one could tell me what it meant. I might be okay in about six or seven months. I might never be able to play soccer again. No one knew. No one wanted to speculate. They all just said, "Wait and see. Give it time to heal. And then you'll know."

All I could think about, over and over, was what had happened to Asher. The ACL tear had ended his career as a soccer player. And mine might be over now too.

It was the worst possible time for this to happen.

Colleges were all starting to make their decisions right now. If I told them I'd partially torn my ACL, no one would pick me up. I'd be history.

So I wouldn't tell them. And I'd wait to see if Sierra woke up.

It was so weird—Kenzie and Joon, side by side, in my hospital room.

Joon knew all about Kenzie, of course. Joon knew everything. And what she didn't know about me, she guessed.

But she'd never really had a chance to talk to Kenzie because everything we did was so private and secret.

I wasn't sure, really, what Joon thought of Kenzie. Joon liked Sierra—a lot. Everyone liked Sierra. She was fun to be around.

The painkillers they'd given me after the accident had made me *so* tired. I felt like sleeping for days and days. But at least my leg didn't hurt.

"There he is!" Kenzie said when I finally opened my eyes.

"Finally, sleepyhead," Joon said. "We thought you were going to sleep forever."

I rubbed the sleep from my eyes. My hand went instinctively, reflexively, to my right knee, where the tear had occurred from the accident. I rubbed my hand over the stitches. Besides the tear, I'd cut my knee up pretty badly too.

"Does it hurt?" Kenzie asked.

I shook my head. "No, not really. The painkillers keep it down to a dull roar."

"Can I see?" Joon asked. She moved closer to the bed to take a look at the stitches.

"What did the doctors tell you about it?" Kenzie asked.

I closed my eyes. The news hadn't been great. "They said I'd have to wait for the swelling to go down, and then I could have surgery. They wouldn't know much until they went in to see the damage. It could be a little—or a lot."

Joon gave me a quick hug. I could see that she was about to cry. "Everything will be all right," she said, her eyes welling up with tears. "I've asked God to make everything better."

"And what did he tell you?" I asked my little sister gently.

"That you'd be fine," Joon said, absolutely dead serious. "And Sierra too."

"Glad to hear it," I said softly, hoping that she was right.

■ ■ ■

The day after the accident, when no one was around, Kenzie asked, "We should tell someone, shouldn't we?" She looked down at the floor.

I shifted my weight in the stiff uncomfortable hospital bed. My leg was beginning to kill me. "Tell them what?"

"You know . . . that Sierra wasn't the one driving."

"Why?" I asked.

Kenzie raised her head and stared at me. "But when Sierra wakes up . . ."

I didn't say anything for a while. "But what if she doesn't?"

I could almost see Kenzie shudder. She knew what I was saying, but it just sounded so . . . cold. So heartless. But it was true. After three days, Sierra hadn't moved a muscle from what anybody could tell.

"Sierra *will* wake up," Kenzie said.

"Okay, well, yeah, I believe that too. And when she does, we'll deal with it then."

"Wouldn't it be easier if we tell the truth now?"

"No," I said, shaking my head. "Because we may not have to. And if we don't have to . . ."

Kenzie shook her head. She was on the verge of tears. "It's my fault." Her voice started to crack.

"No, it's not. You weren't driving."

"But she called me her best friend, and I . . ."

"We," I corrected her. "It wasn't just you who got her upset. We both did. And then I was the one driving."

"I know, but . . ."

"Kenzie, it's all right," I said, not believing my own words. "It'll be all right."

She eyed me. It seemed like there was a deep dark hole between us. "But what if it isn't all right?"

"It will be," I vowed. "It will be."

"But what if it isn't? What do we do then?"

I could see that Kenzie was fragile. This whole thing had really shaken her up. But she had to be strong. We both did.

■   ■   ■

I was in the same hospital as Sierra. But I didn't want to go see her. Not yet. I'd wait until I was stronger.

■   ■   ■

When I was able to walk, I went to visit. It was awful. Her head was a mess, and she didn't move. They'd cut her long hair, which I knew would kill Sierra. The nurses let me stay with her as long as I wanted. But I didn't want to be there. I felt so bad about what had happened.

"I'm sorry," I whispered to her twice. I knew she couldn't hear me. But at least *I* felt a little better saying I was sorry. I didn't know what else to do.

If I'd believed in God, I would have prayed for forgiveness and for Sierra to get better. But I couldn't do that. I didn't know what I believed in right now. And I couldn't very well pray to a God I wasn't sure existed.

For the first time in my life, I was afraid. I didn't know what the future would look like. Not now. I'd always been so certain of the path my life would take. I had it all mapped out, with no detours or roadblocks.

But I didn't know if Sierra would ever wake up. I didn't know if my leg would ever heal or if I'd get that college scholarship. I didn't know if the police would ever find out I was driving and put me in jail for driving without a license and almost killing my girlfriend and her best friend.

None of it made sense. I kept trying to put all the pieces together—or to back up time so we could do it all differently—but nothing worked. I couldn't make it come out right.

Kenzie visited me every day in the hospital. I think she was still in shock, in a way, that she had come out of it with only some bumps and bruises. Sierra was in a coma, and my leg was shattered. Yet Kenzie had walked away unhurt. She didn't know what to think about it. I think it made her feel even more guilty about what had happened.

Two weeks after the crash, Sierra woke

up. No one knew why. She simply opened her eyes, and she was back.

I didn't know whether to shout for joy or cringe at what I knew would be coming next. But I'd had two weeks to think it through, and I'd decided that whatever would be, would be. I couldn't change what had happened. And if and when Sierra came back from her coma, the whole mess would come out. I'd just have to deal with it.

Kenzie and I went to the hospital together. Somehow that was easier. Misery does love company, I guess.

I was braced for the worst. I wanted to see Sierra awake, but I dreaded it too. It was a very, very strange feeling. But I kept my thoughts to myself since Kenzie was freaking out. She was scared that Sierra was still going to be mad.

"Take a breath," I told her as we drove toward the hospital in my Explorer. "You're getting way too stressed out about this."

"And you're not?" Kenzie fired back.

"We don't know how she's going to react, so let's play it by ear. Okay?" I said, trying to calm Kenzie down.

She didn't say anything else until we were in the elevator. And then she started crying. "Ryun, I need to go home."

"It's going to be all right, Kenzie," I said, and put my arms around her. "No matter what happens, we have each other. *Right?*"

I held my breath until she nodded. When the elevator door opened, I watched her out of the corner of my eye. Was she going to fall apart again?

But then something amazing happened. Kenzie sighed and then straightened her shoulders. I've seen that look before, her determined look. It's one of the many things I like about Kenzie. She's tough, at least on the outside. I don't think she lets many people in. Except for me and maybe the kids at the Center where she works.

As we walked down the darkened hospital corridor, I took Kenzie's hand. I could tell she was scared—like the time she'd first gotten on the Yamaha with me.

"Be strong," I said, trying to reassure her. "Remember, it's only Sierra. She's a friend. Not an enemy."

"I know, but what we did . . ."

"Kenzie, give it a little bit of time. We don't know what might happen next. Wait and see. Okay?"

She squeezed my hand harder. "I hope you're right."

"I am. You'll see," I said and then let go of her hand as we turned into Sierra's room.

Sierra had a roommate, an old lady with an odd name, like a state or something. Usually the woman paid no attention to me when I came to visit Sierra. But today I could see and feel her watching us as we entered the room. It gave me the creeps.

Sure enough, just like her little sister, Jacqueline, had told Kenzie, Sierra was awake. She was propped up in bed, one arm still hooked up to the IV. But her eyes were open. I stared at them. They were pretty bloodshot, and you could barely tell they were usually green. But there wasn't a hint of anger in them. She was happy and excited to see us. How could that be?

"Hi!" she said, her voice raspy.

Kenzie jumped right in, rambling on about what friends were saying in school, what Jacqueline and Carin and Holly were saying. I stared at Sierra. I couldn't help myself. She looked so different . . . and I was trying to figure her out. Had she gotten over everything we'd done to her so fast?

Sierra must have felt self-conscious about her hair because she started ducking her head like she does when she thinks her hair is all messed up.

When she called me over to her bedside,

I tried not to drag my leg. But Sierra spotted it right away. "Ryun, your leg! What's wrong with your leg?"

I couldn't believe it. I'd gone behind Sierra's back by dating her best friend, ruined her life, almost killed her in a car crash, and she was concerned about *me*. Sierra had always seemed too good to be true—and here was more proof.

"It's not that bad," I told her. "The brace is just there to stabilize the leg until surgery. . . ."

Sierra's eyes got very wide. "Surgery? The nurse told me you were okay."

"It's not a big deal," I said, trying to reassure her. "I'll be ready in the spring."

That was a lie, one of many I was carrying with me these days. It would take at least seven months to recover from the partial ACL tear, if I ever did recover. But Sierra didn't need to know that right now.

Sierra looked so worried, like it was the end of the world. I couldn't believe she was so concerned about me, considering what we'd done to her.

And I'd cheated on this girl?

At that moment I couldn't face Sierra. I couldn't look her in the eyes. I just couldn't, even though I didn't believe in feeling guilty. It was still too hard. Sierra had gotten the raw deal all around.

When I didn't say anything else, Sierra got all flustered. "I know I don't look great. . . ."

I looked up, glanced around the room at Kenzie, then over at the old lady in the room with Sierra. I was confused. Sierra was worried about her hair and my leg and the way she looked? What about what had happened to all of us on that night?

Kenzie jumped in again. "Everybody asks about you," she said, taking the spotlight off me. Kenzie looked at me. I looked at Kenzie. We both just wanted this to be over, to get it out there and done with.

"I'm so sorry, you guys," Sierra said. "You believe me, right?"

"What?" I said. My head was spinning. This was all so unreal. It didn't make sense. It felt like I had stepped into somebody else's life.

"I'd do anything to get that night back," Sierra continued. "The police said I wasn't drinking."

And then I started to get it . . . and a tiny ray of hope shone through all of this darkness. If the police were asking Sierra about drinking, and she hadn't told them that I was driving, then maybe . . .

"The police? When did you talk to the police?" I asked her.

"Right after I woke up," Sierra said. "I . . . I can't remember anything from the accident. It's all a big blur."

"Nothing?" I asked, amazed. "You can't remember anything?"

"I guess . . . I guess I was driving Dad's car that night, right?" Sierra said. "That's what the police said. Ryun, I'm just so sorry I hurt you. I lost control of the car somehow, and I feel so terrible."

I couldn't believe it. Sierra didn't remember the night of the accident. The police thought Sierra had been driving—and so, apparently, did Sierra. She thought she'd lost control of the car and the police did too. She thought she was responsible for all of it.

Kenzie edged closer to me. She couldn't believe it either.

"Don't you know?" Kenzie asked her.

"No. I really don't remember the accident," Sierra answered, upset. She remembered picking Kenzie up, talking about Taylor and Kenzie breaking up, and some stupid song on the radio. But not the betrayal, not the angry scene on the highway, not the craziness of trying to fling herself out of a car tearing down the highway, not the fiery crash.

I've heard the mind shuts down, like a numbing anesthetic, in the middle of something traumatic. Was that what had happened to Sierra? That her mind had just turned itself off and was slowly coming back on? I wondered if she would ever remember the details of that night.

The police had told her that Kenzie and I saved her life, pulled her from the car before it burned up. She knew that. She just didn't know why. And she seemed so concerned that she might have done something—maybe had something to drink—that might have led to the crash.

"You weren't drinking," I told her.

Sierra was so overwhelmed by all of this, she was having trouble getting the words out. It was so hard for her. "You saved my life. . . ."

Just then the nurse burst into the room and ordered us out. And I was relieved. I wasn't sure what any of this meant. But I knew one thing. If

Sierra didn't remember what had happened that night, I wasn't going to volunteer to fill in her gaps.

Maybe I would make it after all. Get through this. Life took funny turns, and this one was a turn I was going to accept. Without any guilt.

Kenzie always made me visit Sierra. If it were up to me, I might have avoided the hospital altogether. But Kenzie felt so guilty about it all. She wanted to tell Sierra, make things right. I knew she did. But she was also torn. She knew that, for me, it would be best if everything stayed the way it was.

Kenzie knew what would happen to me if it came out that I was driving without my license that night and caused the crash. Especially now—because we'd both let so much time slip by, it would probably be worse. With each day, we were trapped even deeper in our lie.

It was torturing Kenzie to visit that hospital room, knowing everything that she'd done to cause the crash and disrupt Sierra's life. But she faced it, and she dragged me with her each time.

Sierra had missed so much school, she might not graduate with us. I wished there was something I could do about it, but that sort of thing was way out of my league. Sierra's parents would have to deal with the school about it.

I thought the accident would end it for Kenzie and me. Exactly the opposite happened. We grew even closer.

We even went out on a secret date. I knew Kenzie felt a little strange about it. But she went with me, and we had a great time.

A week after I'd gotten out of the hospital, I took Kenzie out for pizza. We went to a place 45 minutes away, where I knew no one from Highview would find us. Still, we were out in public. And I almost didn't care whether anyone found out about us now or not.

So much had happened. And I had no idea what the future held now—for my soccer career, Kenzie, Sierra, anything. It was all one big mess.

It was hard to keep up my act with Sierra, but I knew that I had to. And Kenzie agreed. I had no choice. Until I knew whether her memory of that night would ever return, I had to keep everything steady. Right on course.

And, in the middle of all of it, two weeks before Christmas, Johnny Moser called one evening. No drumroll, no fireworks. Just a call during dinner.

"Hey, kid!" Moser said on the other end of the line. "How's my superstar doing?"

"Great," I lied.

"So are you ready for prime time?"

"Prime time?"

"The ACC, man." Moser laughed. "Playing against all the big dogs—Virginia, Clemson, Maryland, Wake Forest. Are you ready?"

"I'm always ready," I answered.

"Good to hear it," Moser said. "I know you and Asher have talked. So . . . are you ready to commit to Duke? We're prepared to offer you a full ride—tuition, books, room and board. We want you at Duke, Ryun."

I didn't say anything for the longest time. This was everything I'd wanted for so long. I couldn't bring myself to tell him about my leg. Not now.

"Yes, I want to come to Duke," I said at last. "I'll sign the letter of intent when you send it to me."

"Ryun, that's great!" Moser said. "We'll overnight it. We're thrilled. You'll love Duke. I guarantee it."

And that was that. I'd lied. I was going to Duke on a full scholarship. They would give me one of the nine scholarships they were allowed to offer. . . .

I almost felt bad—almost. But I figured Moser didn't need to know about my injury. As far as Duke was concerned, I would be 100 percent by August and preseason. They didn't need to know.

I hung up the phone and turned to my mother. "I will be going to Duke University on a full scholarship," I told her in Korean.

She almost leaped from the table and threw her arms around me. She started to cry on my shoulder. I let her cradle her head on my shoulder. Joon just grinned because she'd thought this would happen all along.

"I am so proud," my mother said, tears of joy still streaming down her face. "You have made me so very proud."

"This is what you wanted?" I asked my mother.

"Yes, it is," she said, still crying.

My mother didn't know, of course, what all of this really meant. But she knew that I had been accepted and honored at one of the finest universities in America. That was all she wanted—and needed—to know.

And, like that, I was back. I could do this. It would be all right. I'd work like a dog to rehab my knee, get it in shape by the start of the summer, play in a couple of tournaments, and be good as new by August.

As long as Sierra didn't mess anything up, I'd be fine.

26

There's this funny TV commercial about a
guy about to go under the knife for brain surgery.
He's joking with his surgeons about what kind of
SUV he drives before they stick the gas mask over
his face. All the nurses think it's funny.

Yeah, real funny. Like you feel like joking with
your doctor on the operating table before they put
you under. That makes a lot of sense.

I had the surgery on my leg the Thursday before
winter break at school. That meant I only had to
miss a couple of days of school.

Joon stayed with me through all of it. My mother
was there too. They were both there with me when
my father took me to the hospital, checked me in,
and then left to go back to the stores.

Joon was there when they talked to me about

the procedure, when they prepped me, when they put me in the wheelchair. She was right there by me. She never left. Joon knew. I didn't have to tell her. She just knew—like she knew everything about me.

I was terrified. I'd never tell anyone else that. But Joon knew me. She knew what this meant to me, what it would do to me if I wasn't able to play soccer again.

I think Kenzie knew too. She was there with me as much as she could. But I think Kenzie also felt guilty about spending too much time with me while Sierra was still stuck in her own hospital bed.

Joon felt no guilt. She stayed by my side every second. She wasn't about to leave me to the dark whisperings of fear and doubt.

"It's not so bad," Joon whispered to me as I opened my eyes after the surgery.

I blinked several times, trying to adjust to the dim light in my hospital room. "What?"

"The scar," she said. Joon was standing beside my bed. I think she'd been there, standing, the entire time, waiting for the instant when I woke up.

But there was someone else there too, someone I hadn't expected—Asher. But Asher had always shown up at times like this in my life.

I glanced down at the bandaged knee of my right leg. "How . . . ?"

"I asked the nurse to let me take a peek at it," Joon said. She reached out and touched my shoulder. "And it's really small. You will hardly notice."

I glanced over at Asher. He smiled. "Girls love

scars, Ryun," he joked. "Trust me. It wins you lots of points."

I took a deep breath. I was almost afraid of asking the question—the one I knew Asher would understand better than anyone else. "So how bad is it?" I finally managed.

Asher pursed his lips. "Not as bad as you might think."

"Really?" I couldn't quite bring myself to hope for the best. Not yet.

"It's a partial tear," he said. "They had a lot to work with. You'll have scar tissue to work around, and we'll need to make sure you do plenty of strength work in your rehab. But I'm hopeful."

"It's not like yours?" I asked him, my voice barely louder than a whisper.

"No, Ryun, it's not anything like mine," Asher said. He came closer. "You're a lucky kid. We'll get the job done. You'll see. It'll be fine. You'll end up with 95 percent mobility. And once I'm done with you in rehab, that particular leg will be stronger than the other one. You have my word."

I looked over at Joon. "So is it okay? Will it all be okay? Did you check with God on it?" I asked her. But this time I was serious.

Joon smiled wanly. "Yes, Ry, it will all be okay. I think Mr. James is right."

"And while you were talking to him, did God happen to mention my soccer career?"

"I think you'll be as good as new, like Mr. James said," Joon said firmly. She believed. And, for Joon, that was all it would take. I wished I could believe it too.

"So you can give Duke the good news," Asher said.

"The good news?" I said.

"That it's just a partial tear and that you'll be back playing by summer," Asher said quietly. "You *did* tell them about it, right? They know?"

"Oh yeah, that," I lied. "I told 'em I thought it would be a partial tear, so they'll be real happy that it's only that. . . ."

I hated lying to Asher, maybe more than to anyone else. But I had no choice, really, did I? I couldn't tell him the truth, could I? Then I'd really have no one in my corner.

I closed my eyes. My knee ached. It was a dull throbbing ache, one I could feel even through the painkillers I was on. "But inside the knee . . . ," I said, my voice trailing off.

Joon leaned over the bed. "Ryun, I promise. It'll be okay. Don't worry. Your leg will be as good as new when it heals. It will be. They just needed to get in there and make sure everything was connected right."

I smiled, despite the aching pain. Joon always hoped for the best. A hurricane could come along, blow our house away, and she'd convince herself that it was fine. We needed a new house anyway. It was one of the things I loved about her. Joon saw hope in places that no one else could.

"If you say so, kid," I managed.

"I say so," Joon said. "It *will* be. You'll see. Good as new."

"Believe her," Asher said easily. "Joon knows. And after I've worked you over the next six months . . ."

I closed my eyes and drifted back to sleep, trying to ignore the pain that hovered right there on the edge of my consciousness. I was glad Joon and Asher were there. I wasn't alone.

27

I had no idea who P. D. James was. But I had to get something for Sierra for Christmas, something that she'd like, so I asked Kenzie.

And Kenzie said P. D. James. She said Sierra loved mysteries and that P. D. James was one of her favorite authors. All I knew was that P. D. James was pretty old and she'd written a bunch of books. How would I know which one to get?

But somehow, Kenzie seemed to know which ones Sierra had read and which ones she hadn't. Girls always seem to know that kind of stuff. Don't ask me how. I have no idea.

Kenzie said to look for one of her newest books, something about justice. The hero of the books was this guy Adam Dalgliesh, who was always able to figure things out, no matter how twisted or complicated.

I was glad Dalgliesh wasn't assigned to the Sierra Reynolds case. I wanted it to remain in the hands of Sergeant McCarthy, thank you very much, who would just leave things well enough alone. It was Sierra's dad's car, so everyone still assumed she'd been driving. And since she'd been the one hurt the most, nobody was going to sue anybody. There was no reason to investigate further. And that was fine with me.

It wasn't hard to find the James book. The bookstore didn't even have to special order it. So I got it, put it in my backpack, and decided to give it to Sierra on Christmas Eve, in the morning.

I couldn't go by in the evening or on Christmas, of course. Kenzie and I had something special planned. It had taken me three days to find the right present for Kenzie and to figure out where to go.

I wished, kind of, that I could plan something special for Sierra. But what? Guilt nagged at me, and I pushed it away. Sierra was stuck in that stupid hospital bed, so it wasn't like we could go anywhere, do anything. P. D. James would have to do.

I knew my present to her, right now, would mean more than anything in the world. Sierra was like that. The smallest of things made her happy.

Kenzie and I agreed that I had to visit Sierra on Christmas Eve morning by myself.

"It wouldn't be right for me to be there," Kenzie insisted. "Not when you're there to give her a Christmas present."

But it'll be awkward, I thought. Any day at the hospital without Kenzie was awkward. And there had been some days where she just didn't want to come anymore. I think it bugged her to see Sierra and me together. But both of us knew there was nothing we could do about it . . . yet.

I had leaned a lot on Kenzie since the crash. But I could get through this.

Kenzie and I had even gone shopping together for Sierra. After suggesting P. D. James for me, she'd bought Sierra a T-shirt with words on the back about backing off. It seemed like a dumb present to me, but I wasn't saying anything. Girls always knew girls. And I couldn't even come up with my own idea for Sierra without Kenzie, so who was I to complain? I sure wasn't about to try buying her shoes.

So on Christmas Eve morning, I went by myself to see Sierra. The instant I stepped into her room, I could see that something had changed. Sierra was different. She was like her old self. Only something was different from her old self. I couldn't figure it out. It was the same Sierra I'd always known. But with something . . . new.

I sat down next to her. "I got the call from Duke, so it's official. Full soccer scholarship."

"That's great, Ryun. But what about your leg?" Sierra asked.

"I didn't tell them about the accident or my leg. I figured—need to know, right?"

"Well, congratulations," she said. But there was a weird look in her eyes, as if she *wasn't* all that happy for me. Or maybe she'd been expecting it, so it wasn't all that exciting. I wasn't sure.

"I picked up something for you." I pulled the P. D.

James book out of my backpack and handed it to her. Just then I realized I should have wrapped it. But Sierra barely looked at the title or the back cover to see what it was about. Instead she seemed intent on studying me. It made me nervous.

"Thanks," she said. "I guess I'll have lots of time to read."

When we talked about graduation and the fact that Sierra may not be able to graduate with our class, I could see the change. Sierra was determined. She would graduate on time. She would come back to school with a vengeance. She would get right back into the swing of things, once she was out of the hospital bed.

So that must have been it. Somehow Sierra had come to terms with what had happened to her, and she was now determined to move on. She was focused on her own path. What others were doing didn't seem to matter as much. Well, good for her. Maybe a little of me had rubbed off on her.

Sierra wasn't a deep person, not by anyone's definition. But there was something deeper here, now, between the two of us.

Kenzie would say it was just the good old Sierra storming back to take charge of her life, to get things right, to start lining everything up again. Kenzie was probably right. She usually was.

But I wasn't sure. Not completely.

Her final words, as I was heading for the door, bugged me. "Ryun? I'll never forget what you and Kenzie did. Saving my life and everything . . ."

And all I could say was, "I gotta go. Bye, Sierra."

"You didn't!" Kenzie started screaming at me.

I confess I was clueless. I had no idea at all what could make Kenzie so mad at me—especially on Christmas Day.

We'd each opened presents with our families in the morning. The only present I liked was Joon's. She'd saved up her money for the entire year and bought me a genuine leather jacket. I was in shock when I opened it. The thing must have cost a small fortune. Sierra had, in fact, pointed one out to me in the mall before the accident. And this one was very similar.

Joon must have spent all of her babysitting money on the jacket. Why? I have no idea. I guess because she loved me, because I was her big brother. And because she was the only one, other than Kenzie, who knew about my Yamaha.

"Joon . . . thank you," I'd said, almost speechless. My mother beamed as she watched me, as did my father. Of course neither of them had any idea what the jacket was for. But they could see the look on their daughter's face as well as I could.

"You're welcome, Ry," my little sister had said, her face turning a little crimson. "Be safe with it, okay? Promise?"

I'd nodded. "I promise," I'd vowed.

But now, later on Christmas Day, exchanging presents with Kenzie at the park, I was totally clueless. What could have made her so ticked?

"I didn't what?" I asked.

"Your present to Sierra!" she yelled, her voice still much louder than it needed to be in the stillness of that quiet Christmas afternoon. We were sitting in my Explorer, in Kenzie's favorite park. It was one of those parks where the occasional dog walker went by. But other than that, we were safe here. It wasn't a place any of our friends or acquaintances would visit.

The P. D. James novel? But she'd helped me pick it out. "P. D. James was your idea," I said. "Why are you getting so bent—"

Kenzie got out of the Explorer and slammed the door.

I sighed and opened the door on my side to get out too.

"*Not* P. D. James!" she snapped. "The other

present, the one Sierra wouldn't show us when we went by to see her."

"What other present?" I asked her, even more clueless. "I only gave her the P. D. James novel, like you and I had talked about."

Kenzie glared at me. Her lips quivered when she got furious like this. One of her eyebrows twitched. It wasn't a pretty sight.

"So you didn't give her something red from Victoria's Secret?" she demanded.

I had to laugh. "Victoria's Secret? Are you crazy?" Like I'd ever visit that place.

Kenzie's eyes flashed. I could see the wheels spinning. Was I lying? Was Sierra lying, making something up to save face because I'd given her such a lame Christmas present?

"She said she'd gotten something red, underneath her hospital clothes. . . ."

"Did she show it to you?"

Kenzie thought for a moment. "Well, no, she didn't show it to us. Carin and Holly were there too. But she was about to."

"But she didn't show it to you?"

"No, I guess not."

I breathed a little easier. I could get through this catfight and come out on the other side looking good. "Okay, then I'm telling you. I didn't give her something from Victoria's Secret or anything else. It was just P. D. James. Nothing else."

Kenzie squinted, still torn about who was telling the truth here. "But why would Sierra tell us she'd gotten something like that from you when she didn't?"

I shrugged. "Who knows? Maybe because she was mad she was stuck in the hospital on Christmas Eve. And because I gave her some book. I'm sure she would have liked something a little nicer . . . and speaking of something nicer . . ." I took a small blue velvet box out of my pocket.

Kenzie eyed me, then took the box. She opened it and gasped, "It's beautiful!"

"And it's for you." I helped her fasten the single pearl on the gold chain around her neck.

I smiled at the look on Kenzie's face. It had taken me a long time to find the right gift—and it had set me back a lot.

Okay, spare me. It had set my father back quite a lot.

And then Kenzie gave me her gift too—a cool brass soccer ball key chain that she'd made herself, with the kids at Little Lambs. I loved seeing Kenzie there with the kids. She was so different—so open and soft, like she was most of the time with me. Not guarded like she was at school.

As the light started to fade on Christmas Day, I held Kenzie's hand as we walked around the park. "Thank you," she said, resting her head on my shoulder. "I love my necklace. I'm sorry about blowing up at you. Guess Sierra was mad—"

"And wanted something nicer," I finished.

Kenzie's face flushed. "Like the pearl necklace you gave me."

"Yes, like the pearl necklace I gave you."

Kenzie looked down. I could tell she felt terrible—

torn between her feelings for me and her loyalty
to Sierra as a friend.

"Okay," she said miserably, "I get it now."

"So you trust me?"

"Yes, I trust you."

But I wasn't so sure.

29

Sierra wasn't released from the hospital until New Year's Eve. After that I stopped by a couple of times. We sat on the couch. It was a little awkward for both of us, but neither of us said anything. It was, in fact, easier for me to talk to her mom than it was to talk to Sierra.

I offered to drive Sierra to school like I always did. But she wasn't coming back to school on the first day. She said she didn't feel up to it.

On the first day back after winter break, I went by to see Coach Jenkins. My crutches were long gone, but I still had to hobble around a little. Because it was a partial ACL tear—not a complete one—I was off crutches and headed to rehab a lot quicker than I would have otherwise.

"So what's the deal, Lee?" he asked when I walked into the office just off the gym.

"Deal?"

"Yeah." Jenkins pointed down at my right leg. Jenkins was a phys ed teacher. He wasn't the most energetic guy in the world. He'd send his classes outside for 20-minute runs at the start of class for their warm-up. Then he'd toss a ball out for some game and let them play for the rest of the class. I don't think teaching was his thing.

The surgery had been a success. The bandages were off. Joon had been right—the scar on my knee was pretty small. The doctors had gone into my knee through a tiny opening and tinkered around with all the stuff in there. I hoped they got everything right.

But the doctors also told me to take it easy. It was possible that I could play a little soccer later in the spring, if I wanted to push it. I didn't. There was no way I was going to risk anything to play for Highview, not if I didn't have to. Not when I had something bigger waiting for me at Duke.

"Oh, my knee," I said, shrugging.

"Yeah, your knee. How is it?"

"It's fine. It's starting to heal."

Jenkins nodded vigorously. "Okay, but when can you start playing again?"

"Soccer?"

Jenkins shook his head. He'd never liked my attitude. But there wasn't anything he could do about it. He'd always needed me. "Yeah, soccer. When can you play?"

I eyed my coach, knowing he wouldn't like my answer. But I didn't feel like lying to him. I had enough of that in other parts of my life. "Coach, I don't think it's going to work out," I said bluntly.

"Work out? What's that mean?"

"I don't think I'm going to be able to play this spring. It's too big a risk."

"The doctors said that?"

"Basically, yeah, they said that."

"So you're not going to play for me this spring?"

"Yeah, Coach, I think I'm done for the spring."

Jenkins tensed up. His face got red, like his head was going to explode. I knew he wanted to reach out, grab me, shake me up a little, tell me I was making a mistake. But he didn't. Instead he glared for an instant, then turned away from me. He got up from his chair and left the office without another word. He didn't look back.

My first day back at school went from bad to worse after Jenkins stormed off. I went to my locker. Kenzie found me. I was starting to describe what had happened with Coach Jenkins when all the commotion started.

"Sierra!" someone yelled.

"Hey, it's Sierra! She's back!" someone else yelled.

I whirled. So did Kenzie. Neither of us had expected Sierra back on the first day.

But she was here, crutch and all. She hobbled toward Kenzie and me. I couldn't read her face. It was a mask. If she suspected something between Kenzie and me, you sure couldn't tell it from her look.

"Hey, you guys!" she yelled at us.

I walked into the center of the hall toward Sierra. After a minute, Kenzie followed.

"I thought you weren't coming to school," I said, picking up her crutch that had dropped to the floor when we hugged.

"I changed my mind," she said.

"That's so great," Kenzie gushed. "You're so awesome to make it here like this. So what can I do to help?"

"Can you get my notebook out of my locker and carry it to class for me?" Sierra asked Kenzie. "It's a little tough on a crutch."

"No prob," Kenzie said. "Whatever you want."

And off we were, the three musketeers. It was totally awkward sitting in class with Sierra and Kenzie, like nothing had happened. When everything *had* happened.

I barely paid any attention to what Ms. Rowe said about the Raymond Carver short story we were reading. I didn't care. Raymond Carver, whoever he was, wasn't going to mess with my future. And besides, I was too busy studying Kenzie and Sierra.

Kenzie was fuming. Sierra was oblivious. She was just happy to be back, in the school where she was queen of the universe. Everybody loved Sierra. They were all thrilled to see her back. The world was right again.

Except it wasn't.

"You know why, don't you?"

"No. Tell me."

Asher gave me his lopsided smile. He'd never gotten his teeth straightened as a kid, so he looked a little like a vampire when he smiled. I liked it. The vampire thing suited him. "Because your high school soccer team is his whole life. And it kills him that you're not available to him."

We were out on the turf practice field, just the two of us, after school that day. The combination of my awful discussion with Coach Jenkins and the miserable day I'd spent watching Sierra hobble around school had put me in a bad mood. I wanted to go somewhere, anywhere, where I felt at home.

And the soccer field, with Asher, was the closest place to a safe home I had on the planet.

I still liked to hang around my club practice,

even if I couldn't practice. Asher, like he always did, was tapping a ball up and down on one foot while we talked. It was his nervous habit.

"But what about what's best for me?" I asked.

Asher shrugged. "I'm not sure he cares about that. Your value is what you can bring to him, to his team. Anything other than that doesn't matter to him."

"That's pretty cold."

Asher stopped dribbling the ball and put his foot on top of it. An amused smile crept over his face. "You can't be serious."

"What?"

"You, of all people . . ."

"What does that mean?"

Asher chuckled. "You're a trip, Ryun. So tell me. When was the last time you looked around at the big bad world and wondered about anything other than what was in it for you, what you could get out of something?"

Ouch. That hurt. It was true, but it still hurt. "Hey, no fair picking on the injured kid," I tried. "You can't do that."

"They didn't operate on your brain, did they?"

"No, but . . ."

"Then I can pick on you. It's allowed." Asher shot a soccer ball in my direction. Instinctively, without thinking, I reached out and trapped it with my other leg, the one that hadn't been injured. "See? You're going to be fine."

I grunted. "Yeah, right. Like they're going to let some gimp play in college."

Asher walked over to retrieve the ball from me and casually put a hand on my shoulder. "Hey, look. It's not as bad as you think. I'll help you every step of the way. You'll be fine. You'll be back by the summer."

"But that means I'll miss all of the team's games this spring. Three tournaments, maybe regionals."

Asher didn't take his hand away. "Ryun, listen to me. I mean it. I'm serious. You will not play another game for me until you're 100 percent. I want you ready to go when you step back on the field for me. And I will make sure you're ready. I give you my word. You'll be good as new by the time you head to Duke."

"You think?"

"I know. You'll deliver exactly what Duke is expecting. I guarantee it. I'm glad they agreed to take the risk on you. Because I know it will all work out."

"Yeah, I'm glad too," I said, wishing I didn't have to lie so much to Asher. "But how can you be so sure about it?"

Asher reached down and pulled the bottom of his sweatpants up, above his left knee. "You've forgotten about this?"

I looked down. The scar on Asher's knee was monstrous, at least four times the size of mine. I had forgotten. "Oh yeah."

"Oh yeah is right," Asher said. "So, remember. I know what you're going through. And I'll make sure you get through it. Don't worry. I'll make sure."

I glanced back down at the nasty scar on Asher's knee. "But you never made it back."

Asher nodded. "Yeah, you're right. I never made it back. But that was 10 years ago. Mine was a full tear—yours is just a partial. And arthroscopic surgery has changed a lot since then. Now they can go right to the problem, fix it, and get back out. You'll see. It'll be okay."

"You're sure?"

Asher didn't waver. "Ryun, I promise. I'll be with you every step of the way. You will recover. I give you my word. And when you're ready, when you're whole again, you will step back on the field, good as new. But not a minute before then."

"Okay."

"But promise me one thing."

"Yeah, what?"

"That you'll focus. Get things right."

I hesitated for a moment. Asher had no idea what he was asking. Or did he? Either way, I had no choice. "Yeah, I will," I answered. "I'll try."

Sierra was driving Kenzie crazy. All Kenzie could talk about was what Sierra was doing or telling her.

I had no idea why Sierra and I were still together. It wasn't the same. Sierra didn't remember the night of the accident, but I did. It was always with us, whether we were together or not.

But it was much worse for Kenzie. She felt so guilty. She felt terrible that we had betrayed Sierra. And she felt even worse that we were still seeing each other behind Sierra's back, like nothing had changed after the night of the accident.

But what was really making Kenzie crazy was what Sierra always said about me. To her. As guilty as she felt about seeing me behind Sierra's back, it was even worse when Kenzie thought about how Sierra and I were still together.

Sierra seemed bent on telling Kenzie how wonderful everything was between us, how we were falling in love, how it was so special. And that we were even closer after the accident than before. None of it was true. I figured Sierra was just compensating, trying to make up for everything she'd lost in the accident.

But Kenzie believed every word from Sierra. Every single word. What was it with girls, anyway? Even after all the yelling the night of the accident, Kenzie still stood by Sierra.

"She's my friend!" Kenzie said, defending her on one of our Wednesday nights. "She wouldn't lie to me."

"But you lie to her," I offered lamely.

"Yeah, but I don't have a choice, at least not for a while."

I told Kenzie over and over—there wasn't much of anything going on between Sierra and me. Not really. We went out together, kind of. We were like two boats docked together in the same port—side by side, but with separate captains. And separate agendas.

Sierra had changed. The accident had focused her in a way I'd never seen. Yeah, maybe it was because she had so much schoolwork to catch up on, so many friends to catch up with. But there was something else. She was paying much closer attention to everything around her. Everything, actually, except me. And that was weird. Because before the accident, she had treated me like the center of her world. Now I was on the outside, like a tiny planet circulating out of range.

But Kenzie didn't believe it. Every time she knew Sierra and I were out together, it about made Kenzie lose her mind. We argued about it all the time.

There were times *I* was ready to give it up. To tell Sierra that it was over. But then Kenzie would bring me back to reality—make me realize how much I had to lose.

Other times it was Kenzie who would insist. "That's it. I'm going to get it over with. I'm going to tell Sierra what's been going on and about the night of the accident." But then she'd stop and remember—how much we both had to lose. In a strange way, we both needed Sierra.

So I kept trying with Sierra. But Sierra wasn't into much of anything. Even when I called her house, I spent more time talking to her mom than I did with Sierra.

The first week we were all back at school, Carin's boyfriend, Greg, set it up—Sierra and I would double-date with Carin and Greg that Friday for the game. But that day Sierra wasn't at school. When I phoned after school, she said she wasn't up to it. That she had a fever again or something.

It was a lucky break. I'd acted like the sweet boy-friend, making sure Sierra was okay. But now I was off the hook. And I could go to the game with the person I really wanted to go with—Kenzie.

The gym was jammed by the time we got there, so Kenzie and I found a spot to hide together on the visitors' side of the gym, tucked away in the corner where I was pretty sure no one would pay a whole lot of attention to us.

I spotted Carin and Greg on the visitors' side.
Kenzie waved to them, and they kept turning to
check us out, in between plays. But other than that,
Kenzie and I might as well have had the place to
ourselves.

And all Kenzie could talk about was Sierra. She
paid no attention to the game at all.

"Then let me break up with her," I pleaded with
Kenzie.

"No!" Kenzie exclaimed. "Not now, not yet. We
have to let her get through everything. We have
to. It's only fair."

I kept glancing out to the floor, semicurious
about the game. The stands were full on our side
and almost full on the visitors' side.

Our basketball team was decent. They seemed
to win more games than they lost, and tonight they
were winning. Everyone was riveted on the game,
stomping and cheering. Everyone except Kenzie.
She couldn't shake loose from Sierra.

"Come on!" I pleaded. "Why can't I just break
up with her?"

"Because. Sierra has to get her life back together,
and you're part of her life."

"But not really."

"That's not what Sierra says," Kenzie said, gritting her teeth. "She talks about you all the time.
You're a big part of her life, and it would hurt her
a lot if you broke up with her."

"Kenzie, give it up," I answered. "I've told you a
million times there isn't anything going on with us.
I'm only going through the motions."

"But Sierra isn't."

I sighed. This was hopeless. I would never convince Kenzie, and I was getting tired of the same conversations. "Look," I said, taking her hand in mine, "there isn't anything going on with Sierra and me. We go out, but we don't even talk much. We just hang out."

Kenzie squeezed my hand back. She glanced around. Everyone was riveted on the game, so she left her hand inside mine and didn't let go. "I believe you, Ryun. I do. But . . ."

"But nothing. You're the one, Kenzie," I said, letting Kenzie's hand stay in mine. Part of me didn't care if anyone saw us together. I was sick of everything. I knew Kenzie was right, that we didn't want Sierra going crazy if I broke up with her. But I didn't care nearly as much as Kenzie seemed to care. Kenzie didn't want to hurt Sierra.

"I know," Kenzie said. Her eyes were all misty. I knew she liked me a lot. That's why she was so torn. She liked Sierra too.

I liked holding Kenzie's hand. I liked leaning in close to her, the way we did just before we kissed. It would be nice if I could do it all the time, just be with her. But I knew Kenzie was probably right. It was too soon for Sierra. We had to let things play out for a while longer.

Two rows down from us, on the visitors' side, I spotted Carin talking, all hyper, on her cell phone. Greg was watching the game, but Carin was yakking away on her phone. Then she did something odd. She got up, started walking in the aisle, and aimed the phone at us. Right at Kenzie and me.

Then I got it. I yanked my hand away from Kenzie. Kenzie jerked, stunned by my reaction. "Hey!" she said, turning to face me. "What gives?"

I tilted my head toward Carin, not wanting her to catch on that I knew.

I was about a second too late, all the way around. Carin had figured out what she was seeing before I could realize it. Then she acted before I could understand what she was actually doing.

Carin's face was blank—I wasn't even sure she was looking at us. But she held the phone aimed at us for a moment longer before pulling it down. Then she returned to her seat and didn't turn around again. I could see that she was fiddling with the cell phone.

I knew, though. There was this sinking feeling in the bottom of my stomach.

I didn't take Kenzie's hand again. The damage had been done. "Kenzie," I said, turning to face her, "I think we just got nailed."

Kenzie gave me a strange look. "What?"

I tilted my head toward Carin a second time and leaned over to whisper in Kenzie's ear. "Carin saw us."

Kenzie glanced down at Greg and Carin. Greg was watching the game. Carin was still messing around with her cell phone, holding it up, playing with it. "Carin saw us? How do you know?"

"She turned around, saw us."

"Do you think she'll tell Sierra?" Carin was really

Sierra's friend. They'd been friends since middle school, maybe longer. She didn't know Kenzie or me all that well. But I wasn't worried about Carin saying anything. It was much worse than that.

"I think she took a picture of us," I said.

"A picture. How . . . ?"

"Her cell phone. She aimed it right at us. I think she took a picture of us holding hands."

Kenzie's eyes got wide as it hit her. "If she took a picture . . ."

"Then she could send it to somebody, if she wanted," I said, finishing Kenzie's sentence.

"And Sierra might see it?"

"Sierra will see it."

33

Which, of course, is exactly what happened.

Carin didn't just e-mail it. She sent it to the world. By the time Kenzie and I got home from the basketball game, it had been attached and e-mailed not only to Sierra, but half of Sierra's friends.

They might as well have put it on the front page of the newspaper: "Heroes Caught Holding Hands!"

Kenzie said two-thirds of her IMs were about The Picture. Everyone was asking her about it. Was she going out with Ryun? Why were they holding hands? Had Ryun dumped Sierra? Why was Kenzie doing this to Sierra? What gives?

I had to laugh. All of the stuff we have—computers that are smarter than us, TVs that find things for us and cut out all the commercials, handheld computers that chart the stock market, navigators in cars that connect to some "voice in the sky" and tell us where we are. And cell phones that take pictures and then send them to your closest friends.

Pictures don't lie, of course. They tell an unblinking story. No amount of talking or explaining gets around the stories they tell.

But Kenzie and I gave it our best heroic effort.

"Not true," Kenzie said in one IM. "R U crazy? Sierra's my friend."

"Just friends," I told everyone.

"Ryun was just being a good friend," she explained to Sierra in an IM. Sierra didn't write back. In fact, I didn't see her online the entire weekend. And that was weird for Sierra, the social director of High High, who was always keeping in touch.

I called Sierra. I got her mom. "I'll pick her up Monday for school," I told her mom, asking her to pass on the message.

■   ■   ■

As I pulled into Sierra's driveway on Monday morning, I wondered what I was in for. I didn't have to wonder long. Instead of waiting for me in the house, like she usually did, Sierra limped out to the Explorer.

"Hey, you're not on crutches anymore!" I said, surprised.

"Got rid of them this weekend," she said. Then, as she fastened her seat belt, she asked, "Have a good weekend?"

Uh-oh, I thought. *Here it comes.*

But she surprised me. She didn't mention anything about the game—or Kenzie. Absolutely nothing. As if it didn't even happen.

"So was it a good game?" Sierra asked breezily.

"The game?"

"Yeah, you know, basketball. That *was* what you were watching at the game, wasn't it?"

"It was okay. The game, I mean."

"Great. So all is well at Highview." Sierra reached over and changed the radio stations until she got a song she liked. She turned the volume up and sat back. I felt like I was in the twilight zone.

But it was a different story at school. All of Sierra's friends gave me the ice treatment. Only Megan approached us as we walked into the school.

When Sierra opened her mouth to talk to Megan, I knew I was in trouble. *Here it comes . . .*

"Megan," Sierra said calmly, "if you're talking about the gossip from Friday night, you can forget about it."

What?

Megan's jaw dropped open. "Forget it?"

"Kenzie and Ryun are friends. They sat together at the game. Big deal. It's just high-tech gossip. Right, Ryun?"

I was no fool. "Yeah, that's right!"

■ ■ ■

The rest of the day didn't get easier though. All of Sierra's friends found me and told me off. The Rumor had gone everywhere, everyplace. Fast.

Holly was majorly ticked. "What's going on, Ryun?"

I explained the same thing to her and later to Carin and everybody else who stuck their big fat nose into it. "We're just friends."

"Yeah, but friends don't hold hands at basketball games," Carin said, her eyes narrowed. She'd seen what she'd seen.

"Hey, Kenzie was upset," I explained. "We were just talking. We've all been through a lot. You guys don't understand."

"Yeah, *girls* sometimes hold hands when they're talking. But a *guy* doesn't hold hands with a girl unless . . . you know," Carin insisted.

"No, I don't know," I tried. "Tell me. Why can't a guy and a girl just be friends and hold hands?"

"Right. Yeah, whatever." Carin smirked and turned her back to go. Holly gave me the look of death and followed Carin down the hallway.

And, of course, they were right. I *was* blowing smoke. But it was the only weapon I had, so it didn't hurt to try.

I didn't know any guys who held hands with girls because they were friends. You held hands with girls because you liked them. But, hey, you have to do what you have to do sometimes. And this was one of those times.

And what amazed me is that, every time, Sierra took my side. Just when I was expecting a bomb to drop on me, Sierra would come rushing up. "Ryun was only being a good friend to Kenzie. There's

nothing going on. Nothing to worry about. I'm glad they're friends."

To all that, Carin, of course, simply raised an eyebrow.

"It's high-tech gossip," Sierra told Carin.

By this point I was beginning to wonder about Sierra's sanity. What was going on? Was Sierra so desperate to hang on to me as her boyfriend that she'd look the other way on something like this? Was she just acting like the old Sierra, wanting to make the best of everything?

I knew that Carin didn't buy it. Not many would. I mean, come on!

But what did I know about the inner workings of the female mind? I just dated girls. I was thankful I didn't have to figure them out too.

Kenzie didn't believe me.

"How could you?" she said. When Kenzie got worked up like this, her voice started to crack and get raspy.

"But I didn't."

"Sierra said it, for a fact. You told her you love her, that you'd been talking a lot since the accident and since she got back from the hospital and that you were getting closer and closer."

"Kenzie, you know it isn't true. . . ."

Kenzie had just about had it. More and more, she talked about giving it up, going public. I didn't say anything when she got in one of those moods. I wasn't sure what made sense. Part of me didn't care. But the other part of me wanted to hang on to the charade for as long as possible—at least until I was sure we were clear of trouble.

Today was worse than usual for some reason. Kenzie had waited until there wasn't anyone around our lockers, and she had practically pinned me up against them. Her face was inches from mine as she whispered fiercely, not really caring who heard her words.

"*How* do I know it isn't true? How? Sierra tells me one thing, and you tell me another. Sierra's been so nice to me since the accident. She's been an awesome friend."

I glanced around nervously. Our faces were so close, and Kenzie was getting so emotional that I was sure someone would notice. "Hey, come on! It's me. You know I haven't—"

"I *don't* know," she insisted. "That's what bothers me. I don't know."

I knew it wasn't true. Sierra and I were going our own separate ways. I could see it. I knew it for an absolute fact. Sierra was changing. She was different, not in a way I could explain to anyone. Not in a way that would make sense.

But she was. I knew it. Sierra was a different person than the girl I'd met before the accident—deeper, more introspective, more thoughtful. She seemed to have more layers to her than I'd thought. She was clearly going through some stuff. I had no idea what. We didn't talk about it.

In fact, we didn't talk at all. When we went out together, Sierra always made sure someone else tagged along. At first it was Carin and Greg. Then after Carin dumped Greg, it was Carin and some guy Mick. I barely knew Mick, but Sierra dragged the two of them around with us at every opportunity. It was like she was afraid to be alone with me.

I didn't care. It was just as well. I didn't have the heart for endless window-shopping and long discussions about the latest fashion in shoes. That wasn't my thing. I only put up with it when I had to. And I was beginning to wonder how much longer I had to put up with it. It was getting old. And Kenzie was the one I wanted to be with anyway.

Kenzie, of course, saw none of this. She seemed clueless about Sierra's changing heart. She only saw that Sierra seemed to be paying pretty close attention to what Kenzie was doing, more than she had before. Kenzie loved it—and hated it—at the same time.

There was one other thing too. Kenzie kept saying that she thought Sierra knew more about the accident—that more of her memory had returned—but wasn't saying.

I thought Kenzie was paranoid and a little spooked because everything had turned out all right for us. But I kept my mouth shut about it. No sense in making Kenzie any crazier about everything than she already was.

"Kenzie, I don't know what to tell you," I said, shrugging. "You know I'd never tell Sierra I loved her. I wouldn't. Ever."

Kenzie leaned closer. "But you've never told me that . . ."

"Hey, guys!" Sierra's loud bubbly voice rang out in the hallway.

Kenzie's head whipped back.

I blinked once and turned. "Hey, Sierra," I said,

a tight smile curling up the corners of my lips. I had this weird feeling that Sierra had been watching, waiting for this moment, and then waded right into the middle of the two of us. But that would have made me paranoid too. And I wasn't going for that. Plus, I'd never known Sierra to be able to think that far ahead.

"You guys looked awfully intense. What's up?" Sierra's limp was gone, and the bounce was almost back in her step. She closed the distance between us in short order and took up her usual position as close to me as possible. When we were in public.

"Oh, just stuff," Kenzie answered, glancing down at her feet.

Sierra slid her left arm around my waist, tucked her head into my right shoulder, and took hold of my right arm with her right hand. It was a 100 percent Sierra gesture.

Kenzie looked up, saw it, and a look of murder flashed across her face.

"Hey, Kenzie, anything wrong?" Sierra asked sweetly.

"I'm fine," Kenzie said, the anger still evident in her voice.

I wanted to pull away from Sierra, but I couldn't. Sierra had me trapped from every conceivable angle.

"You sure?" Sierra pressed.

"I'm sure. I have a couple of tests coming up I'm not clear on. . . ."

"And you thought Ryun could help you with them?" Sierra turned and looked up at me. If I didn't know better, I'd think Sierra was playing with me.

"Yeah, I was going over with Ryun what I had to do. No big deal," Kenzie said.

Sierra continued to gaze up at me with big wide eyes. "Hey, Ryun, so is it all set?"

"Set? For what?" I answered, clueless as usual.

"You know, silly, for Valentine's Day?"

"Valentine's Day?" I was totally confused. What was I supposed to be doing now? How much money would I have to steal from my father this time to cover Sierra's new scheme? I could only imagine.

"You know, you *promised*," she said. "You said you had something really, really special planned for us on Valentine's Day, that it was a big secret and you'd let me know soon."

I glanced over at Kenzie. If looks were daggers, I'd be on the way to the ER right now. "Um, well . . ."

Sierra hugged me tight, squeezing hard. "Oh, I get it," she said, laughing. "That's what you and Kenzie were talking about, and I walked right into the middle of it. I'll bet Kenzie is helping you plan it, and I almost spoiled it. Sorry!"

When Sierra let go, I was incredibly relieved.

I couldn't help myself. I glanced down at Sierra. She was starting to become her usual self again. Her hair was growing back. She'd found a nice way to put it up that made her look cute again. Her wardrobe was killer, as usual. Sierra was back and again queen of her universe.

But there was more going on here, more than just her hair and her outfits. I knew it. I could sense it. Sierra was *thinking.* Observing, watching, and wondering about life.

It was startling, in a way, to see it. And, you know, even though I didn't seem to be part of it, I approved. It was a good thing.

Sierra was coming to life in a way I'd never seen before. Had the accident changed her that much?

"Sierra, it's not that big a deal," I said, not entirely sure what to do. If I told Sierra she was crazy, that would make Kenzie happy. But I'd be toast with Sierra. And if I told Kenzie that I wasn't planning something for Valentine's Day with Sierra—which I wasn't—and that Sierra was just being her delusional self these days, I knew Kenzie wouldn't believe me.

I couldn't win. So I kept my mouth shut.

"Oh, Ryun," Sierra said with a big smile, "of course you don't think Valentine's Day is such a big deal. Guys don't get it."

"Guess not," I answered.

Sierra turned to Kenzie. "But we know better, don't we, Kenzie? We know the truth, don't we? We know *exactly* how things work. Right?"

They were simple words. But they made me uneasy, like there was an edge to them. Maybe I *was* getting paranoid after all.

"She knows!"

Kenzie was frantic. Beside herself. I couldn't tell what was upsetting her more—the thought of me planning some romantic interlude with Sierra for Valentine's Day or her continued insistence that Sierra knew more than she was letting on.

"Okay, look," I said, trying to be patient. "If she knows, then why? Why put up with the charade? Why not come out and confront us? It doesn't make sense."

"She knows," Kenzie muttered, more to herself than to me. "I can tell. Guys are so . . . so dumb about things. They never see it."

I had to laugh. "Are you talking about me? Dumb?"

"Yeah, you. You're in your own perfect little

world, where nothing ever goes wrong and you always win. Ryun the Invincible."

"Hey," I said, softer now. "Kenzie, it's me. I'm not the enemy."

We were in our place at Highview, the one spot where we were sure no one would stumble on us—sitting on the balance beam that no one used except during gymnastics in the crummy auxiliary gym at one corner of the school.

Kenzie reached over and took my hand. "I know. Sorry. I didn't mean to jump all over you. It's just that . . ."

"I know, but you're wrong. Sierra's idea of planning is picking out her wardrobe for tomorrow morning. It doesn't go anywhere after that. You and I both know it."

Kenzie hated it when I trashed Sierra like this. But she also didn't go out of her way to defend her either. Sierra was her good friend. But Kenzie knew I was right about Sierra. And she also knew that every lousy thought or word about Sierra took me one step further away from Sierra—and a step closer to Kenzie.

I reached over and kissed Kenzie. I liked kissing her. In fact, I couldn't think of anything I'd rather do than stay somewhere and kiss her. I could spend hours with her—not talking, just holding hands, kissing. I liked being with her, even as crazy as she made me sometimes.

I felt no guilt about it. For some reason, it seemed like a game when I was with Sierra. It was like a challenge—I had to make it work with Sierra. With

Kenzie, it seemed right. I didn't have to work at anything with Kenzie.

Yeah, Kenzie wasn't as cool or as cute as Sierra. No one was as cute as Sierra. That's what made Sierra who she was and why everybody loved her. She had the market cornered on cute and adorable. And she made people feel good.

But Kenzie was real. She was like Joon—she knew me, even if I didn't tell her everything. And Kenzie accepted me for who I was, no questions asked.

I'd been wondering for some time whether I ought to get it over with. Break up with Sierra. Let the chips fall wherever they wanted to fall. I could do it. I wanted to do it. I wanted to get it out in the open with Kenzie, not hide it anymore.

It was actually Kenzie who kept me from doing it. Although she felt bad about keeping us a secret, she also kept telling me that it would destroy me if it came out now that I was the one driving on the night of the accident. With my suspended license, my entire house of cards would come crashing down around me.

So we kept quiet, Kenzie and me. But it didn't keep me from thinking about it. If I had a little more courage, I'd do it. I'd break up with Sierra and tell everyone I was with Kenzie. And maybe I would. Maybe I'd go ahead and do it.

"So what's your big plan?" Kenzie asked after she'd pulled back from our kiss.

"What?"

"You know, your big Valentine's Day plan."

I shook my head. "I have no idea. Sierra's crazy.

I have no clue what that was all about. She must be desperate for everyone—especially you—to think everything's great with us."

"So you *really* don't have some big Valentine's Day thing planned?" Kenzie couldn't help herself. She continued to torment herself with the thought that maybe I was double-dealing both of them—telling Sierra that I loved her and planning romantic things, and then telling Kenzie that none of it was true.

"Look, I'll tell you what. I'll just take Sierra to The Lantern on Valentine's Day. Okay? I hear a couple of others are going too. How about that? Is that unspecial enough for you?"

That part was true. At least three couples we knew were going to The Lantern for the half-price special. That was even better for me. It meant I didn't have to steal as much money from my father this way. I'd have to pay for the half-price special ahead of time because that was how they guaranteed full seating for Valentine's Day. But it would be worth it.

It also might be a nice time to let Sierra down easily. I could start to tell her that evening that we were drifting apart, going different paths. Which was kind of true. I hardly knew what Sierra was up to anymore.

Kenzie smiled for the first time that day. *"Unspecial* isn't a word."

"Yeah, but it applies here, don't you think?"

"I guess." She slid across the balance beam and deliberately crashed into me, knocking me off the beam. "But I wish you were taking *me* to The Lantern. Not Sierra."

I looked up from the floor, pretending to be hurt. "That can be arranged. Just say the word and I'll drop Sierra. You know I will."

Kenzie let herself fall off the balance beam. She leaned over and whispered in my ear, "Maybe later. Not until we're sure it's safe."

36

Kenzie really loved the day-care center where she worked. She loved working with the kids and teaching them guitar. She loved the fact that she could use her creativity to make a difference in their lives.

She'd worked there with the kids for years, since her mom was the director. Little Lambs was a special place for her. When she wasn't with me, there wasn't anywhere else on the planet she'd rather be. I'd even gone there a couple of times, as a "friend" of Kenzie's, to teach the kids some soccer moves.

And then the shoe dropped. But it didn't land on me. It landed on Kenzie.

■ ■ ■

The Sunday before Valentine's Day, I drove to
Kenzie's house to pick her up, as we'd planned.
But Kenzie wasn't there. In fact, no one was. After
I'd waited about 45 minutes, I left her a phone message and then headed to the Crow Bar for the rest
of the night. It was weird. It wasn't like Kenzie to
blow me off.

■ ■ ■

The next day I drove Sierra to school, like always.
But I didn't say much. I couldn't help thinking about
Kenzie, wondering if she was okay.

As soon as we got inside the school, I scanned
the hallways. Kenzie had to be around here somewhere. No luck. Finally I leaned over to get my
lit book out of my locker. When I stood up again,
I spotted Kenzie. She was already at her locker,
across from mine.

"Kenzie?" I called.

She took a book out of her locker, then closed
it. When she looked up for a second, I saw that
her eyes were red, like she'd been crying. And she
looked like she could cry more too. But instead
of walking toward me, she took off down the hall
toward lit class at a half run.

I don't think I heard a word Ms. Rowe said the
entire class. I was trying to catch Kenzie's eye. But
she didn't look up, and she didn't say a word. And as
soon as the class bell rang, she hurried out the door.

I followed her. Kenzie wasn't acting like Kenzie. I was worried. Something had to be majorly wrong.

I cornered her in a hallway before she got to her next class.

"What is it?" I asked. "Are you okay?"

And Kenzie started to cry. It took me a few minutes to piece together what had happened.

"Somebody told the Little Lambs board . . . that I'd been drinking and taking drugs. . . . They decided they had to investigate," she managed to say through her tears.

"But you don't do any of that stuff," I said.

"I know, but it doesn't matter." She took a breath. "Mom says the board won't let me help with the Valentine's event this coming weekend." She looked up at me. Her tears had streaked her mascara across her cheeks. "And I might never be able to go back."

It wasn't fair. Kenzie loved those kids, and it was clear they loved her. And now because of some silly rumors, Kenzie couldn't do the one thing that mattered to her most—work at the Center.

Sometimes life stinks. And this was one of those times. Worse, there was nothing I could do about it.

37

Oh, man, was I beginning to dread it. A long night alone with Sierra at The Lantern on Valentine's Day. I couldn't think of anything worse—especially when Kenzie was feeling pretty rotten.

I was so not looking forward to it that I started trying to think of lines I could use during dinner, like, "Sierra, I think the accident has changed us, maybe caused us to grow apart a little. I think we need some time apart to sort things out."

Okay, I guess not. But I was getting desperate. I felt trapped. I knew I didn't want to be with Sierra anymore. But I couldn't walk away, not yet. Not until I was certain that everything would be all right. That she wouldn't get all weird on me if she did remember who was really driving the night of the accident.

And yet I knew it was over with Sierra. It was dead. They just hadn't called in the coroner yet.

When I got to The Lantern that night, I waved at Carin and Mick. Greg was there with his new girlfriend, off in another corner of the restaurant. I spotted at least 10 seniors from Highview, huddled over their half-price Valentine's Day dinners.

God, I thought to myself, half as a joke, half seriously, *if you do exist, now would be a good time to help me out. I don't want to be here. I don't want this. Can't deal with it. So please take this away from me. Please.*

I checked on the reservation. I was on the list— two for 7 p.m. for Ryun Lee. Now I only needed Sierra to show.

Sierra always showed up on time. But not tonight. And she'd insisted that I meet her here, instead of my picking her up. When it hit 7, I tried calling her house. No answer. Then I tried her cell. No answer.

When it was 7:30, I tried Kenzie, thinking she might know what was going on. No answer.

At a quarter till 8, when I was standing near the entrance of the restaurant, about to give up on the evening and drive by Sierra's house, Kenzie walked in and started to scan the room. She was dressed to kill, in the kind of dress that almost guaranteed every guy in the place would stare at her secretly from his table when he could get away with it.

I was surprised. *Who is she here to meet with?* I wondered. *And why didn't she tell me she was coming to The Lantern?*

Then she spotted me and smiled. She began to walk toward me.

"Hey, sorry I'm late," Kenzie said when she reached me. "I hurried to get here."

"You're not late," I said. "Sierra's the one who's late. So why are you here?"

Kenzie came up close, so she could whisper to me without being overheard. "Sierra called. She said she's not feeling well. She asked me if I would sit in for her, because she knew you'd already shelled out for the meal ahead of time."

"She did?" I asked, wondering why she hadn't called me to let me know. I checked my cell phone. It was on. It had been on for the entire time.

"She did." Kenzie leaned over to whisper in my ear again. Just the smell of her made my heart beat faster. "And I'm glad. I wanted it to be *me* here with you tonight. So I'm glad. Really glad."

I glanced around the restaurant. Sure enough, Carin was staring at us. It wouldn't take long for this to get around. From the minute we took our seats, it would all start again. The rumors, the talk. The whole deal.

I felt that surge of relief sweep across me again. I'd wanted out, in a big way. I'd wanted to be free and clear of Sierra, so I could be open about Kenzie and me. And here it was, big as life. Right here, front and center. All I had to do was sit down at the table with Kenzie and it would be over. Once and for all.

I took Kenzie's hand in mine and smiled at her. "Let's go," I said, and led her to the table.

Kenzie didn't let go of my hand. Half of the Highview kids in the place saw it. I could see them talking. I knew it would be out on the Net within the hour. Kenzie and Ryun together at The Lantern. On Valentine's Day.

"Alone at last," I joked when we were seated.

Kenzie glanced around. "Is it . . . is it okay?"

Kenzie was nervous. I was relieved. "I think so."

"And you're not mad?"

"What? That you're here, instead of Sierra?"

"Yes, that."

I leaned across the table, aware that at least half a dozen pairs of eyes were following my moves. "Not only am I not mad, I'm glad it's you here with me tonight and not Sierra."

And that was that. It was done. I didn't care. It was just as well. I couldn't have dragged it out much longer with Sierra anyway.

If Sierra was going to hang us, she was going to hang us. Or, to be more precise, she would hang me. Kenzie was an innocent bystander. She'd stand off to the side of the gallows. It would be me making the long walk over to the platform.

38

For the next couple of days I tried to call Sierra. But she didn't come to school, and she didn't return my calls to her cell phone. Whenever I called her at home, her mom politely told me Sierra wasn't available.

For the rest of that week Carin, Holly, and about a dozen other girls all asked the same thing over . . . and over . . . and over again. Was it true? Had I broken up with Sierra? Had she broken up with me? How could I have taken Kenzie to The Lantern? How could I? Why was I so mean?

By Monday of the next week I still hadn't heard from Sierra, and I'd had enough. I stationed myself by Sierra's locker and waited for her.

Right before our lit class was supposed to start, Sierra came in with a bunch of girls.

"Sierra," I called. I tried to walk toward her, but the other girls cut me off. The message was clear. Sierra wanted nothing to do with me. But I wasn't letting her get off that easy. I wanted this over with, but I wanted a clean break too. "Why didn't you call me back?"

Alyssa shot me a nasty look. "Leave her alone, Ryun."

I didn't give up. "Sierra, we need to talk. Why are you mad at me?"

"What did you expect?" Sierra hissed back at me "That I'd be okay with you having Valentine's dinner with my best friend?"

I started to stammer something, but she cut me off. I'd never seen Sierra so mad.

"You could have waited to break up with me first before having dinner with Kenzie."

Wait a second. My mind raced. "But Kenzie said you *wanted* her to have dinner with me."

"Yeah, right." Sierra sneered and then headed for lit class.

I stood still, like a tornado had hit me, trying to process it all.

■ ■ ■

By the end of the day, it was clear to everyone that the Ryun and Sierra era was over, killed on— of all days—the Day of Love. We were broken up for good.

I was glad it was now done. Time would tell if Sierra had something else in mind for me, now that we were no longer together. And I was okay with that.

But Kenzie was crushed. She tried about a million times the first few days to tell everyone that Sierra had asked her to go to The Lantern in her place. Not a single kid believed her. Holly had read her the riot act and said she no longer wanted to be Kenzie's friend. Finally, at the end of the day on Monday, Kenzie told me that she had found Sierra in a group of girls and confronted her.

Sierra denied it all. She said she'd never asked Kenzie to go in her place and that she was really truly hurt that Kenzie would go out with her boyfriend, to *their* place, on Valentine's Day. Even if Sierra was sick and couldn't go, Kenzie should never have gone out with her boyfriend instead.

Kenzie was a mess. She cried the whole time she was telling me this. She felt totally betrayed by Sierra, and now she was an outcast in Sierra's group. But I wasn't a bit surprised. There was something weird going on inside Sierra's head, and it wasn't the usual girl-stuff madness that makes guys crazy. No, this was some serious, marble-rolling-around-inside-the-head kind of stuff. I had no idea what was going on. And, to be honest, I wasn't sure I wanted to know.

39

So, over the space of a weekend, Sierra and
I became ancient history. The word had spread far
and wide that Sierra and I had broken up.

It was so strange. I mean, Sierra and I had dated
for almost 10 months. And then it was over. Gone.
Poof. Next.

I kept expecting some monstrous shoe to drop.
I could feel it coming. I was waiting for Sierra to
lower the boom.

But there was nothing—only sneaky whispers
about how hurt Sierra was. Poor, poor Sierra. First
the accident, then dumped by her boyfriend. It was
all so cruel, so unkind, to sweet Sierra.

At least four girls told me they would never talk
to me, ever again, for what I'd done to Sierra. Of
course, by the end of that first day, two of them had
found me, yet again, to tell me that they weren't

talking to me. I guess they wanted to make sure I knew. It was amazing how the world of rumor and gossip worked. Simply amazing. I guess I hadn't paid attention to it before, because I'd never been involved enough to care.

Kenzie and I hadn't even had time to plan for it. Everything had happened so fast. It was one big blur.

And now everyone assumed that Kenzie and I were together. We hadn't told anything to anyone. Not one thing. But everyone talked. Everyone assumed.

As for Sierra? I only saw her once the rest of the week. I think she was going out of her way to avoid me—and Kenzie too. But toward the end of the week, when Kenzie and I were standing by my locker, we both heard the distinctive *clack-clack* of her shoes at the same time. Kenzie looked up, then quickly down.

I stared in Sierra's direction. Her face was blank, so masklike that I couldn't tell what she was thinking. She didn't even look at me first. She eyed Kenzie.

Then, after a moment, Sierra looked in my direction. But her eyes were vacant black holes. She looked right through me, as if I wasn't even there.

■　　■　　■

But as spooky as Sierra had been, I still wasn't prepared.

"Sit down," Principal Waters said. "We have something to tell you."

This was it—I knew I was in trouble now. I'd been called down to the principal's office and was waiting outside when Kenzie showed up too.

She looked at me with questions in her eyes, but I only shrugged. I didn't want her to know how nervous I was. When the principal's door opened, two police officers—the same ones from the accident—had been standing inside. I was sure we were about to be hauled to city hall, questioned, booked, and taken to jail.

Then they talked to us about a school assembly on Thursday. But what does that have to do with us? I wondered.

As the facts started to sink in, I couldn't believe it. They were going to honor us, Kenzie and me, onstage at Highview High—with all the high schoolers and the middle schoolers watching. And Sierra was going to give the big speech, about how we'd saved her life when we pulled her free of the burning car.

Life is so weird sometimes. Just when you think it's going one way, it makes this sharp right turn and goes in another direction.

I was so sure Sierra was planning something for me. But nothing had happened, even though more than a couple of weeks had passed since Sierra and I had broken up. And then this awards thing came up.

"We thought about surprising you," Sergeant McCarthy said. "But then we decided that might not be nice." He chuckled.

I began to smile. I couldn't believe my luck. Everything had turned out all right. I was free. Sierra and I had broken up, and she was okay with that.

She hadn't turned on me. I was in the clear. Sierra had even volunteered to say nice things about Kenzie and me! Go figure.

In fact, they said, Sierra had helped plan the event with those two cops, Sergeant McCarthy and the other officer. Williams, I think. They said she was behind the whole thing, all the way.

I could finally relax and focus all of my energy now on one thing—getting ready to play soccer again.

40

Asher and I had been working out

together. I was actually beginning to believe—really
believe—that I would be able to get all the way back.

It had been almost three months since the surgery. I had almost full range of motion in my leg.

I was lifting weights almost every day, and I
could feel my leg getting stronger with every passing day. The scar was so small, you almost couldn't
notice it. I might even be able to bluff my way past
the Duke coaches in my freshman year, that I'd had
the scar for years from some stupid skateboarding
accident or something like that.

Asher had begun to work with me on my form
and sprinting in the past two weeks. I was so
thrilled to be outdoors, back on my feet. It didn't

even bother me that I was missing key tournaments, like the Jefferson Cup in Richmond. I had my college scholarship. I was happy to be running again, almost ready to go back out on the pitch again.

"Again!" Asher yelled at me. He was merciless today. We were running wind sprints at half speed. He was making me do all of them with an exaggerated lift and thrust. He wanted to see me get my knees up high as I ran. When I let them drop, he screamed at me.

Asher ran every sprint with me. He did every exercise. He did what I did, at the same pace. And if I slowed down, even a little, he pushed me.

"I'm an old man," he said. "I can't believe you're letting an old man beat you."

"You're not old," I grunted.

"But I'm slow and out of shape. I can't believe you're letting an out-of-shape guy like me beat you all the time."

I pushed that little bit extra, to make sure I got to the line ahead of him. I beat him by half a step and dropped both hands to my knees, pulling the bottom of my shorts down over both knees.

"Not done," Asher said, grabbing my shirt. He pulled me back to the line. "Two more."

I didn't say anything. Dragging myself back to the line, I took off when Asher took off. I stayed with him and edged him down and back. I was gasping for air after both sprints.

Fortunately, so was Asher. "Okay, hotshot, five minutes. But then we're going to shoot. With your bum leg, gimpy."

"Hey!" I protested. "I'm not limping. Haven't you noticed?"

"Yeah, but you're weak, out of shape, out of form. Basically worthless as a soccer player right now."

I grunted again and flopped to the ground.

Asher sat down nearby.

"Do you really think that?" I valued Asher's opinion, more than he knew. I trusted Asher with my life, like I did Joon. I knew Asher would always be there for me, no matter how badly I mangled things.

"No, I don't," Asher said easily. "But I'm not laying off, not for a long time. By the time I'm done with you, you'll be good as new. Better than that, actually. I'm going to make sure your leg is better than it was, stronger than it was before the accident."

"Is that possible?"

Asher nodded. "Yes, it is. We're applying every form of isometrics to it that I can think of. We're strengthening it from every conceivable angle. It's going to work. I give you my word, Ryun. You're going to be fine."

I believed him. I would believe almost anything Asher told me. "And if it isn't? If I can't play again?"

"You'll play again, better than you did before the injury," Asher said forcefully. "Don't worry. It'll all work out. Duke will be very, very pleased when you show up for preseason."

"I know you believe that."

Asher gave me that look. I knew it was coming.

"I do believe that. And I also believe that things happen for a reason, to test us."

I rolled my eyes. "Not again. Not the God-tests-us-for-a-reason speech."

"Okay." He laughed. "But it doesn't make it any less true."

"I believe in what I see, right in front of me."

"Fair enough," Asher said. "But what you see right in front of you—like a soccer ball waiting to be pushed to one side or another around a defender—is a test. You've been given one of your first big tests in life, Ryun. We'll see how you handle it and what it means."

"I'll handle it fine," I said angrily. "And what it means is that I'm going to come back even stronger than before, like you've been saying for weeks."

"Good." Asher nodded. "I want that. But you should also think about why it all happened, what it means."

"I don't care why I got hurt or why I got in that wreck. I just want to get on with my life, work through it. *Conquer* it."

Asher looked at me for the longest time. I could see what he was thinking. I knew it almost as well as he did.

To Asher, my greatest strength—my unchanging faith in my invincibility and my ability to get past any obstacle—was also my greatest weakness. Because it blinded me to what might actually mean something in life.

I didn't care. I wasn't letting anything—not even the possibility that God might exist and might even have plans for my life—get in the way of what I had to do.

"Your call, Ryun," Asher said. "I want you strong. Always. I never want you to back off from anything. Never slow down, never give in."

"I won't."

"But there is a very thin line separating confidence from arrogance, and intensity from insanity. If you cross the line, you're stupid—and a jerk."

"Gee, thanks."

Asher laughed. "Just promise me that, every so often, you'll think about why."

"If you say so, loser," I said.

"You know, you are one big royal pain."

"But you love me, right?" I shot him my best grin.

"Yeah, Ryun," he sighed, "I love you."

"Like a brother?"

"Like a *little* brother who will never, ever beat me in anything."

I hopped up off the ground, ready to go again. I'd had enough talking. It was time to start working hard again. "Let's go shoot. I want to blast a few past your lame attempts to stop me."

"Not with that gimpy leg, you won't," Asher said, joining me.

Asher still believed I'd told Duke about the injury. I hoped—with everything I had inside me— that Asher would never know any differently. I only hoped that I'd be back, 100 percent, by the time anyone got around to asking. By then I didn't think it would matter. I'd be back on the field, ready to roll again. Same old Ryun Lee, on top again.

41

I couldn't help myself. I'd parked the
Yamaha since the cop had pulled me over. I was a
little afraid of driving it, since that night had been
the beginning of my slide. Enough. No way was I
letting anything push me around again. I didn't care
if I got 173 tickets, flipped the bike, and somer-
saulted 83 feet into the air, I wasn't letting anyone
tell me how to live my life. I knew how to live it—
full-out, no fear, no worries. There was no other
way. There was no other choice.

So I'd gone to visit my old friend again. I looked
down at my right hand, the throttle hand. My hand
trembled slightly. The Yamaha's engine roared to
life, the throbbing sound filling the silence around
me in a rush.

The tunnel seemed darker and blacker than it

ever had before. Demons and goblins and who knows what else lurked inside. I didn't care. I was headed straight into that darkness. Into it, and through it, as if nothing had changed.

As I wheeled the bike around and headed toward the tunnel, the tires skidded a little. The controls felt a little awkward to my touch. The bike shimmied a little. The engine sputtered briefly.

"STOP!" I yelled at the top of my lungs and gunned the engine. The bike almost jumped out from under me. I held on for dear life and hunched over the front of the bike quickly to right myself. The bike shot like a bullet toward the opening of the tunnel.

I hit the opening much faster than I ever had before. I was almost at 60 early in the tunnel, while it was still light. I kept the throttle open wide, not slowing down. I was doing this. I didn't care what happened. I was doing this. I wasn't slowing down.

The bike was going so fast now that I couldn't hear a thing except the terrible roar of wind past my ears on either side. The darkness closed in on me. I had to be almost at the bike's maximum speed. Who knew how fast I was going?

But I wasn't paying any attention to that. I had just three thoughts—*keep the bike straight, don't let up on the throttle, and keep your eyes focused on that pinpoint of light to aim for at the other end of the tunnel.* Everything else was a blur.

And then it happened—that one tiny slip that would mean nothing at a normal speed, in a normal environment. But this wasn't normal. And a slip—

any little slip—at this speed, in this place, meant disaster.

The outside of my left handlebar caught the side of the tunnel. And the one small bump was enough to shower orange sparks all around me. For a moment, panic and fear swept through me.

I was going to die. The bike was going to tilt, flip, and turn into the sides of the tunnel. I'd roll and crash in a long slide of fire and grinding metal.

The sparks cascaded and danced all around me, like tiny fairies. The light from the sparks illuminated the inside of the tunnel, casting a flickering shadow before me. One more slip, and it would all be over.

Every muscle I had fought it. I would not lose control. I would not. No matter what, I would ride straight and true. I would not die, not this way. I fought every urge to panic, which would have caused me to lose control of the bike. I would get through this. I would hold the bike up, by sheer force of will.

The bike held its course. I had a death grip on the handles, my legs pinned hard to either side of the bike to keep it stable. I didn't catch the side of the tunnel again. I continued to hurtle forward, toward the ever-widening point of light at the other end.

I ripped out of the other end of the pipe with such force that the front wheel of my bike shuddered, almost causing the bike to flip yet again. But it landed and stabilized, and I held firm. The bike started to slow as I eased off the throttle. I started to breathe again an instant later. Every muscle in my body ached from the effort.

When the bike had slowed to 60 and was on level ground, I lifted both hands from the bike and raised them high in the air. Only the angels—and demons—were there to witness my uncertain victory.

42

Kenzie was really spooked by the awards ceremony. She was so sure. She said she *knew* that Sierra was going to do something to us onstage in front of almost every kid at Highview gathered for the assembly.

Kenzie still believed that Sierra knew more than she was letting on. I don't know how or why she'd gotten that in her head. I just thought she was still paranoid.

Sierra had gone away quietly. I hardly saw her in school anymore. In fact, she avoided me. She'd gotten on with her life, which was fine by me. That left me plenty of room to hang out with Kenzie publicly, with no fear.

Kids still said things. Some of Sierra's best friends, like Carin and Holly, continued to tell me that they were never going to speak to me ever again. They kept coming up to me at lunch, in between classes, just to make sure I knew that.

"Sierra's still mad at you," one of them would say to me in the hallway.

"I know," I would answer quietly.

But I wondered if Sierra really was still mad at me. I think she'd been looking for a way out with me as well. We'd drifted apart a long time ago. Only the accident had somehow reconnected us again, in a way that I think neither of us wanted.

I didn't know Sierra. I thought I did—once. But not now. Gone was the girl who could window-shop for expensive shoes at any time, any place. And replaced by what? I wasn't sure. I didn't know. She was more of a mystery to me now than when we'd first met.

Kenzie and Sierra, of course, no longer hung out together, like they had before Valentine's Day. But in that strange world that only girls inhabit, they still spoke to each other. They remained part of this circle of friends that engaged each other in this dance that I had no understanding of and no desire to learn about.

How could girls do that? They were friends, then they were enemies, and then they were friends again. They hated each other, then loved each other, then tolerated each other. They spread vicious gossip about someone, then yelled at you the next instant for spreading lies about the very same person.

I kept Sierra on my IM buddy list. But I didn't ever send anything to her. She never sent anything

to me. We'd get into these weird three-way discussions, where she'd be talking to someone, who would then send me a message.

But even that died off eventually. She wanted nothing to do with me. That was obvious.

Which was why I thought Kenzie was plain crazy.

"Sierra's over it," I told her the morning of the assembly. "She's moved on. Don't worry. It's okay."

We were in our place, the auxiliary gym. Kenzie had said she wanted to talk. "She's not," she said forcefully. "I know it. She's planning something."

"What? What could she be planning?"

"I don't know. Something. When she's onstage, maybe she'll tell everyone what really happened."

I wasn't worried. "No way. Why now? Why didn't she say anything earlier, if she knew? Why wait until now?"

"Just a feeling. You know Sierra hasn't been the same . . . since the accident. You and I both know it."

"Yeah, I guess. But that doesn't mean . . ."

"Ryun, you *know* that Sierra is still mad at both of us. And if she ever remembered what happened on the night of the accident, don't you think she'd do something about it?"

I sighed. This was old news. "Maybe, but I also think she would have done something by now. I think we're all right. I think we're past all that. I really do."

Kenzie shook her head. "We're not. I know it. Sierra's planning something, and I'm afraid we'll see it at the assembly."

I ducked behind the gym before the assembly, back behind the woods, and smoked a cigarette. I took long careful drags on it, drawing the smoke deeply into my lungs. An instant later, I could almost feel the nicotine coursing through my blood. Calm. I wanted to be nice and cool and calm. I popped a breath mint and headed back to the gym.

The gym was almost full. Most of the kids from Highview were there, glad for any excuse to get out of class. They thought it was a big joke, of course. This was the kind of thing adults were into. It sure wasn't something kids thought about.

Mayor Cellars was up onstage when I got there, along with Principal Waters and the two cops who'd first arrived at the scene of the accident after Kenzie and I had pulled Sierra free from the burning car.

I took a seat beside Kenzie onstage, right next to the mayor. Just for kicks, I asked the mayor whether he liked his job. He gave me that politician's smile— the one that seems plastered on the face, rain or shine—and said sure, why not. He didn't seem real happy to be here. Not enough voters in the crowd, I figured. I wasn't paying much attention to him, either. I was mostly watching Kenzie and trying to keep an eye out for Sierra, who wasn't there yet.

A minute later, Sierra stepped onstage. Principal Waters rushed up to her. "Great! You're here!"

I didn't want to seem obvious, but I watched Sierra out of the corner of my eye. But I couldn't read her.

Sierra was even more distant than usual today. She took a seat well away from Kenzie and me, near the police officers. She glanced once in our direction and managed a tight smile. I nodded once quickly and turned back to Kenzie. I wasn't afraid of Sierra or what she might do.

But Kenzie was worried. She was so nervous I thought she'd start shaking in her seat.

I reached over and touched her arm. "Relax," I whispered. "It'll be okay."

"No, it won't," she whispered fiercely. "You'll see."

My friends out in the crowd gave me a few high fists, saluting me. I returned the salutes.

Not a single guy in the school cared in the slightest about what had happened between Sierra and me. No, scratch that. They cared that Sierra was available and that they could ask her out. That was the extent of the caring. A few guys had checked with me after Valentine's Day to make sure it was true and that they could ask Sierra out.

"Knock yourself out," was my usual reply.

But Sierra hadn't been out with anyone since we'd broken up, at least not that I could tell. I'd seen her talking to guys but hadn't heard of any dates. For Sierra, that was really weird. She was known for always having to have a boyfriend.

I also heard from Carin and Holly, when they were talking to me, that Sierra's friend from the hospital—the lady with the name of a state, Missouri—had died recently. They didn't know much about it, only that Sierra had been pretty broken up about it. And that Sierra had gone earlier that day to Missouri's church for a memorial service.

But all of this was distant thunder. I didn't care who Sierra went out with, and I hardly knew what was going on in her life. I guessed she must have gotten close to that old lady in the hospital if she'd wanted to go to her memorial service. You know, it was strange. I used to know everything about Sierra—she used to talk to me nonstop. Now I knew nothing. But I wasn't going to sweat it. I'd come out okay, and it looked like Sierra was doing fine too.

Principal Waters practically gushed about how happy he was to see the mayor. It was pretty disgusting. Then Officer Williams gave his account of the dramatic rescue—minus the part about my losing control of the car and wrecking it, of course. The mayor said a few nice things about Kenzie and me and gave us each a silly plaque. I had a nice place all picked out in my closet for it.

And then it was Sierra's turn. "Come on up, Sierra," our principal said.

It was as if someone turned a light switch on. The crowd went quiet. Everyone seemed to edge forward in their seats. Then a buzz started again.

Maybe Kenzie was right. Maybe there was something here that I didn't quite see. Clearly Sierra's friends were waiting for something, even if only a few sharp unkind words aimed at me, the guy who had wronged her.

I turned my attention from Sierra's friends to Sierra. She looked nervous. I'd never thought of the queen of Highview as the kind of kid who got stage fright. But she was definitely uncomfortable, no question.

I glanced over at Kenzie. She'd slid forward to the edge of her seat. Her eyes were narrowed to slits. She was watching every move Sierra made.

Sierra got to the mike and just stood there. There was a long pause. She looked like she was struggling. The principal tried a stage whisper, to encourage her to start speaking. The mike picked up his words, and the crowd started to laugh.

Then Sierra spoke. Everyone leaned forward, waiting to hear.

"A lot's happened since the accident, to all of us—Kenzie, Ryun, and me," Sierra said, her voice almost cracking from her nervousness. "Not everything has been easy. Or good."

These words were not coming easily. Not at all.

"Memory's a funny thing," she said after another long pause. "There's a lot I want to forget about that accident. And a lot I want to remember. Someone really wise once told me that life is about remembering the right things and forgetting the wrong."

Sierra paused again. Kenzie was so rigid and tense beside me I thought she'd break in half. I almost turned and looked at Sierra. But I didn't. I was afraid that, if I did, she'd let all her anger toward me spill out onstage. So I didn't move.

"There are a lot of things I'm going to try to forget," Sierra said after this second longer pause. "But I want to remember that you pulled me out of the car. Thank you."

Then she stopped.

There was this awkward silence and then some sputtering applause. The principal dismissed everyone, and the place emptied in a hurry.

Very weird. Kenzie turned to me as Sierra began to exit the stage. "She changed her mind," Kenzie said, gritting her teeth. "I know she did."

"What . . . ?" I started to ask, but Kenzie had already left.

Someday, *maybe,* I would understand girls. But right now, I didn't care in the slightest. I just had this funny feeling that I'd escaped something— again.

44

"... you know!"

Kenzie was hot. She'd caught Sierra just before she could leave the stage, and she was physically keeping Sierra from walking down the stairs. I kept my distance and eavesdropped. They were practically nose to nose. I'd never seen Kenzie so animated or so angry.

"You haven't lost your memory," Kenzie continued. "You've known all along about the accident. . . ."

Sierra smiled weakly and told Kenzie that she didn't want to play anymore.

I couldn't believe it. Kenzie had been right. Sierra knew. She'd always known.

That meant she'd gotten her memory back right after the accident, after she woke up. She remembered it all—the conversation between Holly and

Kenzie in the bathroom, the confrontation in the car on the way to the pizza parlor, the tears on Route 58, how she tried to open the door while the car was moving, the fiery crash as I lost control.

She remembered it all and knew the many degrees of betrayal that both Kenzie and I were responsible for. I couldn't believe that Sierra—dear sweet Sierra—had carried this with her for this long. It was so . . . not Sierra.

And I knew that she had almost certainly done something about it over time. Now I wasn't sure about anything—*had* Sierra been getting even? Was that even possible with someone like her? Was it?

But an even bigger question, really, was why. Why didn't she tell us she had her memory back?

Revenge. That had to be it. We had betrayed Sierra, and she needed time to get even. But in the end, the sweet part of Sierra had somehow won out. She hadn't been able to go through with it, for whatever reason. She'd had enough. Decided it was finally time to forgive and forget. No more games.

"You did it, didn't you!" Kenzie practically yelled. "You got me fired from the Center. I knew it. I knew it was you!"

"It was. I'm sorry," Sierra told her former best friend. "I was just so mad at you for letting me take the blame."

Kenzie was almost trembling with anger. "What was I supposed to do? I didn't lie. The police assumed you were driving. And Ryun let them. He was driving without a license."

Sierra glanced over at me. "Why?" she asked Kenzie.

"His license was suspended," Kenzie answered. "I should have known that you didn't know that."

I'd heard enough. The ball was headed in my direction, and I knew I'd need to defend myself.

I reached Kenzie's side and touched her shoulder. "Everything all right?"

"Everything is *not* okay," Kenzie said. "Sierra hasn't lost her memory. She's been faking it the whole time."

I put on my own version of the politician's polite smile. "No way. She couldn't have faked that."

Sierra looked at me finally. I guess she wanted to make sure I heard this. No need. I knew. "I did lose my memory, at least at first. But I got it back in the hospital."

I let the smile drop, though not the casual attitude. There was no way I was letting Sierra see that any of this had gotten to me. Never in a million years. "Have you told the police?" I asked her.

I could see the anger in Sierra. It was there, everywhere, as she explained about why she wanted revenge so badly. She wasn't going to the police, she said. But she had done some damage.

"I've done some things, Ryun, some things I can't undo," Sierra said. "I wanted to hurt you. I've talked to Duke. I told them about your injury."

I put a protective arm around Kenzie and told Sierra that Duke wouldn't believe her. But I knew they would. My scholarship was gone. I just had to wait for the ax to fall.

"You know what? I'm not buying into any of this," I said, more for Kenzie's benefit than anything else.

Sierra looked genuinely sorry for an instant and at a loss for words. "I'm sorry. Be careful," she told me, and then pushed her way past Kenzie and me and left the stage.

45

Asher was merciless, as always, at practice that evening. I wasn't sure how Sierra had pulled it all off, knowing all along what had happened on the night of the accident and plotting her revenge all this time. How had she carried it with her for so long?

Kenzie was still so angry she couldn't even think straight. I felt bad for her. She was almost an innocent bystander in all of this. Yeah, she'd gone out with me behind Sierra's back. There was that. It wasn't good.

But it wasn't like she'd been the one driving that night without a license. All along she'd only been trying to protect me, without hurting Sierra too much. She'd even tried to do the right thing on the night of the accident by getting it all out in the open with Sierra.

I decided I had to come clean with Asher, in between our sprints. To tell him the whole story about dating Sierra and Kenzie—well, at least most of it—from start to finish, because I had a sneaking suspicion I'd need his help. I left out the drinking and smoking part, of course, but left in as much as I dared with him.

Asher thought it was, well . . . funny. "So you got crushed by a girl," he said.

"Not like, you know, crushed . . ."

"What would you call it then?"

I thought for a moment. "Well, nothing has actually happened yet."

Asher was really enjoying himself now. "So you thought you could get away with it—dating two girls at the same time . . . ?"

"And best friends at that," I interrupted. "At least according to Sierra . . ."

"Right. Which, of course, blew up in your face. It made one of them so crazy that she tried to throw herself out of a moving car and caused this huge wreck, hurting herself badly and mangling your leg."

"Which I've recovered from," I added.

"Which you *might* recover from," Asher corrected. "You're not back. You're getting there, but you haven't proven anything. Not to me, just yet."

"But I will."

"Okay, but here's the deal. This girl, Sierra, has cleaned your clock. You ever think she might be the one responsible for the picture of you and this other girl that you were complaining about way back in the winter?"

"Yeah. And it's pretty clear she set up Kenzie and me for Valentine's Day."

"So is there anything else?"

I really didn't want to tell Asher this next part. But I had no choice. Not now. "Well, I didn't exactly tell you the truth about something."

Asher turned toward me. He had a curious look in his eye. "Duke?"

"Yeah, Duke. I didn't tell them I got injured."

"I know," Asher said quietly.

"You do?"

He sighed. "Yes, I do. But I was waiting to see if you would tell me yourself. Moser called me a few weeks ago to go over the training he wants to see from you this summer. It was clear to me he had no idea you'd been hurt."

"Did you tell him?"

"No, I didn't," Asher said. "But you should. It's the right thing to do."

I looked down. "Well, it doesn't matter now. I'm pretty sure Sierra told Duke about my injury."

Asher looked genuinely sorry for me. "What about the smoking and your fake ID and—"

"Hey!" I said loudly. "I never said anything about smoking or fake IDs."

Asher cocked his head to one side and gave me that look. He had this annoying habit where he squinted one eye and glared at me with the other. It spooked me.

"You're such an idiot," he said. "You thought

I didn't know? What do you take me for? I
know more about you than you know about
yourself."

"Hmmm," I grunted.

Asher pointed a finger at my chest. "So I'd say
there's no contest here. This girl, Sierra, crushed
you. She let you off easy today on that stage, not
turning you in."

I got very quiet. I looked up at Asher. I needed
his help, now more than ever. "You know they're
going to take my scholarship away at Duke, now
that Sierra has told them about my leg?"

"Yep," Asher said bluntly. "You lied to them.
There's no chance they won't yank the scholarship.
And they're right to do so."

"So what do I do?" I pleaded with him. "What
can I do?"

"You really want to know?"

"Yes, I want to know."

Asher looked at me before speaking. I knew it
was coming. The speech. Asher couldn't help himself, really. He'd missed his calling. He should have
been a preacher. It was his job.

"Okay," he said. "You need to get everything
right with God. Come clean with yourself and him.
No more lies, no more risks, no more deceptions,
no more betrayals. You need to get it all out in the
open. God will forgive you if you admit you need
help. If you're honest about everything you've done
wrong. There isn't a sin in the world he hasn't seen
before. I promise. But it all has to come out in the
open. Every last bit of it."

"You really do sound like a preacher," I said, subdued. Part of me wanted to believe what he was saying. I wished it were that easy.

"I'm sorry. I don't mean to," Asher said. "But I'm telling you the truth. It's the best thing. You've got to get rid of all this stuff, and then— and only then—can you move on to make better decisions. There is no other way. You can fool everybody. But you can't deceive God. It doesn't work that way."

"But what about college? Even if I believed in God and I asked him to forgive me, it's not like he can find me another college scholarship."

"Yeah? He can't?" Asher said, laughing. "You really think that little of God? You don't think he can turn something like that around?"

"You know what I mean," I grumbled.

"Ryun, I do know what you mean. But I'll make you a deal. You sort these things out, get things squared away, and we'll talk. We'll work out a plan, how to approach colleges this summer with the full picture. Everything. Your injury, your driving record, the whole thing. We'll find the right opportunity, and we'll make it work. I give you my word."

I almost believed him. I wanted to believe him.

It would be so nice. No lies, no stealing, no deception, not ever having to worry about who you told your last lie to and what you had to avoid in the next conversation. Just live your life with no fear of being caught or found out. Wouldn't that be great?

Yeah, it would be great. Too bad it wasn't likely to happen—at least to me—anytime soon. I was in way too deep. It was a long way back, and I wasn't ready to begin that journey.

46

Kenzie called me about 50 times on my cell. I didn't answer any of them.

After practice, I decided I didn't feel like thinking about much of anything. Not Sierra or Kenzie, not school, not soccer and my injury.

What I wanted, more than anything else at that particular moment, was a drink. A nice double scotch, just ice, at the Crow Bar, with friends who knew nothing of Highview, of Sierra, of my scholarship at Duke. That's all I wanted. Give me a little oblivion and I'd be happy.

When I got there, four of my friends were already there. "Ry!" they called, then slid a chair over for me. I ordered a drink, put it away, and ordered a second. My friends gave me strange looks but said nothing. They could see I was here for one reason—

some serious drinking—so they left me alone. They'd been there before.

By the third scotch, I was happy. No more Highview, no more Sierra, no more trouble. Just these guys and their own various troubles and plots at work. My head was spinning a little. I was afraid to speak. I knew what I'd sound like if I tried.

I thought I felt a tap on my shoulder, but most of my body was numb. So I shrugged it off. Then a second tap came on my shoulder.

One of my friends pointed at me and then to a spot behind me. I turned in my seat.

Sergeant McCarthy—Sierra's Sergeant McCarthy, the Sergeant McCarthy from the accident, the Sergeant McCarthy from the awards ceremony at the assembly today—was standing behind me. He folded his arms and looked down. There was no mercy in those eyes. None.

"Young man, you're in serious trouble," Sergeant McCarthy said.

The men around the table slid their chairs back a little. Not a single one of them came to my defense or even bothered to ask what was going on. They wanted no part of this, whatever it was.

"I am?" I managed to say. "Why?" I knew my words were slurring. I knew I was well on my way to getting drunk. But I couldn't do anything about that now.

"Can I see your ID?" he asked.

"My ID?"

"Yes, your license. Can I see it?"

I fumbled around in my back pocket for my wallet, panicking now. What should I do? Give him my real license, which was suspended? Give him my fake ID? I couldn't think straight. It was all a little too complicated at the moment.

Sergeant McCarthy made the choice for me. As soon as I'd pulled my wallet out, he spotted the fake ID. "May I?" he asked, reaching down.

I pulled the ID from my wallet and handed it to him. "It's fake," I said, suddenly wishing I'd heeded Asher's advice a little sooner.

"I can see that, young man," he said. He peered at the ID, then at me, then at the men around the table. They all looked away, guilty.

"You all should know better," the sergeant said. None of them said anything. He was right. They should have known better.

Sergeant McCarthy glanced back down at my wallet. Even from his vantage point, he could see that it was overflowing with cash. "Can I see your wallet?" he asked politely.

I almost stuffed it back into my pocket, out of view, but thought better of it. I was in deep. I had no idea what the best thing to do was here—sit tight and try to hide everything, or let whatever was going to happen, happen. I handed him the wallet.

He opened it, saw the amount of money inside, and whistled. "That's a lot of money for a young man your age. What did you do, rob a bank?"

"I, uh, I . . ." Then I stopped talking. There was no way I could explain it. I didn't have a job. If I said I did, it would take all of two seconds to ask my folks about the job, and then he'd know. My folks would know. It would all start. My house of cards would tumble down completely.

So I shut up. I looked up at Sergeant McCarthy and didn't say another word.

"Okay, I get the picture," he said quietly. Even in my deluded fuzzy state, I could see the sadness in his eyes. It wasn't anger. It was something else. Pity, maybe, or disappointment.

"Let's go, son," he continued. "I'm taking you home. You can explain everything there."

I dare anyone to try it some time. Just try it. It is, without question, the longest loneliest ride on the planet, sitting in the backseat of one of those threadbare police squad cars, dreading every turn of the wheel as you head toward home.

I should have listened. To Joon. To Asher. Even to Sierra. But I hadn't listened to any of them. I was just so sure I could get by. I'd always gotten through everything without a scratch. I'd always been untouchable. Invincible.

Until now.

I was almost sober by the time we got home. Sergeant McCarthy rolled his windows down as we drove along the streets, letting the cool fresh air blow through the car. By the time he walked me up the drive, I was almost thinking clearly again. Fear can do that. Sober you up in a hurry, I mean.

"Son?" Sergeant McCarthy said as we neared my home. "Are you ready for this?"

"No," I said truthfully.

"You do know how much trouble you're in. You do know that, right?"

"I guess," I said. "But I wish it would all go away."

"I'll bet you do," he said. "But you should have thought about that some time ago."

He escorted me to the door and knocked. My father answered the door.

"Mr. Lee?" Sergeant McCarthy asked.

My father looked at me, then at the policeman, then back at me. He turned without a word and ordered Joon and my mother off to another room. I knew Joon would stick around, listening. I had no idea at all what my mother was thinking just now.

I knew it was over. The masquerade ball was coming to a close. Never mind my scholarship at Duke. I might be going to jail. I wasn't exactly sure for what—a fake ID, stealing from my father, driving with a suspended license. I had no idea what they all added up to . . . except for a whole lot of trouble.

"Mr. Lee," Sergeant McCarthy said, "your son is in quite a lot of trouble."

"I think I can see that," my father said, his voice almost emotionless. "Can you tell me what he's done?"

My father listened quietly as Sergeant McCarthy explained what he'd seen at the bar, what he'd found in my wallet. My father didn't look at me, not once, the entire time. He kept all of his attention focused on the police sergeant.

When the sergeant was done, my father turned to me. His eyes were unblinking. "Is it true, what this man has said?" There was no accusation in the tone. Only the question.

I closed my eyes. *I will not cry. I will not. Not here, not before my father. Dear God,* I thought bitterly, *how have I gotten here, to this place? How? And what do I do now to make it all go away?*

A quiet unexpected peace seemed to settle on me, the kind of peace I'd never known before. Asher's words were there, right before me. I could almost reach out and grab them. I knew what I had to do.

"Yes, Father, it's true," I said, opening my eyes and looking straight at him. "I have deceived you, our family, my friends. I have stolen from you, and I have done things I should not have done. I am sorry. Very sorry."

And with no thought for the future—what it might mean, what the consequences might be, now or later—I told my father and Sergeant McCarthy the truth. I told them everything, holding nothing back.

Asher would have been very proud.

"I can't believe you told them everything," Joon said, clearly in awe.

She'd slipped into my room after I'd finished telling my father and the police sergeant my tale of woe. She must have been on the stairs and heard the whole story. Actually, I was glad. It meant I didn't have to lie to Joon anymore.

"I can't believe it, either," I said, plopping down on my bed. The room had almost stopped spinning.

Joon was such a nice kid. Nothing got to her. I don't think she was surprised at all by what she'd heard. Maybe the stealing. But not the drinking or the smoking or the fake ID or the driving without a license. She'd already guessed all of those long ago.

I wish I would have paid attention to her words— "Be safe"—when she'd given me the leather jacket.

Then I wouldn't be in this mess. And my mother wouldn't be in her room, crying. And my father wouldn't still be standing in our living room with Sergeant McCarthy.

"I didn't want to tell you, not right now. But maybe now is okay," she said. Joon had her hands behind her back. She was still standing at the foot of my bed.

"What?" I asked, looking up at her, not sure there could be anything worse waiting for me at the end of this long road.

Joon held out one hand. There was a slip of paper in it. It had two words written on it and a phone number. Johnny Moser, Duke's assistant coach, had called earlier in the evening, when I was at the bar.

"Great," I said, looking down at the bedcovers. "Now it's all done. In one day. Everything. My scholarship's gone."

Joon started to cry. I couldn't believe it. What was it with girls, anyway? I'm the one who gets crushed, as Asher would say, and Joon's the one crying?

"It'll all be okay, won't it, Ryun? You'll be okay?" she asked me, her lips trembling, the tears spilling onto the carpet in my room. I hated it when girls cried. It about killed me. It made me feel so helpless.

"Hey, c'mon," I said, lifting my head up. "You know me. I'll be fine."

"Really?" Joon said, wiping away the tears on one cheek.

"Never fear. It's all good." I stopped and smiled. I couldn't believe I'd just used Asher's words—the ones that used to drive me crazy. *It's all good.* I continued, "I can make it through this."

Joon walked over and leaned close. She gave me a quick hug—something I usually hated. But this time it was okay. I didn't mind so much, because it was Joon. She would always love me, no matter what I'd done. She wished only the best for me and never thought the worst of me. Not even now.

"You know I've been praying for you for a long time," she said.

"I know," I answered.

She lifted her head to look at me. "And are you gonna stop?" she whispered. The fear in her voice was real. I knew that she'd wanted to ask me this for a very long time. But she'd never had the courage, not until now.

I looked up at my little sister. "I'll try. I will. But no promises, okay?"

Joon nodded and stopped crying. As long as I was willing to try, she'd be happy. "Start with the cigarettes, okay? Those things are so nasty."

49

There would be no jail time. At least not
the physical kind.

My father didn't file charges against me for
stealing money. That kept me out of juvenile hall.
That means I wasn't a criminal in the eyes of the
law. But it would be a very long time before my
father trusted me again. And I couldn't blame him.

Two days later, with Sergeant McCarthy watching nearby, they threw the book at me in district
court for continuing to drive after my license was
suspended. Evidently the cops had interviewed
Kenzie, and her written statement had been the
final nail in my coffin.

I'd be a grandfather, I figured, before they gave
me my license back. How was I supposed to manage?

"That's your problem," my father had said. "Figure it out."

And that's exactly what he'd left me to do. Only I noticed that my father was home now at dinner each night and that he expected me to be there too.

My entire life had to change. Even though I was now eighteen, my mother had to drive me to school. My parents and I agreed that I had to come home straight after school with Joon if I wasn't going to practice with Asher. Sometimes I felt like I was in middle school again.

I stopped playing soccer on Sundays with my adult friends, of course. It would be a cold day in you-know-where before I patronized the Crow Bar again.

Smoking was the hardest part. Go figure. Who knew that nicotine had such a hold on you? I was sure I was going to die. For four straight days, all I did was wander around, craving a drag on a cigarette. I couldn't think of anything else. All I wanted was to feel the rush of the nicotine.

This too passed. But I knew, in some corner of my mind, that the craving would never go away. I would always want a cigarette. Forever. The pull was that strong.

Joon was the one who helped me through this part. Every morning she came into my room, woke me up for school, and asked me if I wanted a cigarette.

"Yes, badly," I answered four straight mornings.

"Too bad, 'cause you can't have one," she said to me for four straight mornings.

I didn't sell the Yamaha. For some reason, I couldn't part with it. Maybe it was because some

part of me still wanted to dream. But I did keep my bike helmet—for that day when I was middle-aged and able to ride again. I'd already promised Joon that she was the first person I'd take on a ride—and not through the tunnel, either.

I did, however, sell the Ford Explorer. I gave all the money from the sale to my father, to help pay for what I'd stolen from him. When I'd given it to him, he'd simply bowed, accepted it, and looked at me. For the first time that I can remember, I saw a glimmer of emotion in my father's eyes. "You are my son," he'd said, "and you will always be my son."

But I knew I could never truly make amends for everything I'd done. My mother was still in a state of shock. I wasn't entirely sure she believed what my father had told her. But she believed enough. She didn't speak to me for two whole days—just started to cry every time I saw her. But thanks to Joon, my mother and I talked. And it got better. It would be okay. I was her best son again.

There had really been only one more little surprise. But it was no surprise at all, I guess. Not really.

Kenzie broke up with me too—the Saturday after the awards assembly. She had asked me to meet her at our park. I went to talk. Kenzie went to run away—from me. I guess I didn't blame her.

And, finally, there was Sierra. Of all people, of all things, of all the truly crummy things I'd ever done, I felt worst about Sierra. She hadn't deserved what I'd done to her—dating her best friend behind her back and putting her in the hospital. Most likely she would never forgive me, not really, not for all the pain I'd put her through. And I couldn't blame her.

I wished—man, I really wished—I could do something about it. I wanted to tell her how sorry I was. But Sierra wanted nothing to do with me. She'd steered clear of me at school. And she was always surrounded by her "crowd," who seemed to be protecting her from me.

I knew I might never get the chance to tell her. It was the way it would have to be. Forgiveness was a tricky thing. I knew that now. But I hoped that somehow, deep down, she would remember the "I'm sorry" that I'd whispered to her twice in the hospital . . . and know I meant what I said. Then and now.

50

It was a clear, sunny, brilliant day. Not a cloud in the sky. The kind of day to be outside, running circles around your opponents on a soccer field.

Joon didn't say anything to me for the longest time on the drive to the soccer tournament. We both sat in the backseat, while my mother drove.

Joon knew how important this game was to me. Everything else had been stripped away. All I had left was this game and the huge gnawing doubt inside me that I could ever measure up again.

It was about a two-hour drive to the soccer tournament. It was my first since the accident and the injury. Asher had continued to punish me with rehab every day for weeks, and then made me wait an extra four weeks after that to make sure I was totally ready to go physically. Only my state of mind was suspect now.

Joon broke the long silence halfway there. "It doesn't matter, you know."

"What?"

"How you do today," she answered. "Whether you score or not, how you play. It doesn't matter. You have time. You'll figure it out."

I smiled. Good old Joon, ever the optimist.

But I needed to know for myself. I would find out today what was possible. I would find out whether I had thrown away the talent God had given me. The talent I had ignored and taken for granted so long.

"Thanks, Joon," I said. "But I need to know what's left."

"I know you do," she said. "But I have faith in you, Ry. I know you can handle this." I could only hope she was right.

It took me an eternity to warm up and get loose before the game even started. Everything seemed foreign to me. I felt like an alien on my own planet.

"I'm scared," I admitted to Asher before the game. "What if I don't have it?"

We were playing some no-name team from somewhere in eastern Pennsylvania. We'd played them once a couple of years ago. I'd handled their marking backs easily. I was at least a step faster than them.

But that was then. Before the accident, before the surgery, before all the rehab. Who knew what would happen now?

I hadn't played a competitive soccer match for almost seven months. I had worked my tail off with Asher every day, for the better part of two months, to get back to where I was.

But I had no idea—none—what would happen when I tried to turn on the speed in a match, or what might happen when I tried to cut back on my injured leg. I wouldn't know until I tested it. And I was terrified. It hadn't sunk in until now, this very moment, that I might be finished as a soccer player.

The years of work and sacrifice. Thousands of hours of wind sprints and finishing. Endless hours of drills and moves in a vast array of defensive possibilities.

All for nothing—if I could no longer reach that extra gear when I needed it, or that sharp cut at the exact moment when the marking back was poised to strip the ball from me.

Asher was right. He'd been right all along. I *had* taken God's gift for granted. I *had* wasted. I *had* taken the talents given me and believed my own lie.

But I hoped—almost prayed—that there was still enough time to find that gift again. With everything else gone in my life, it made it very easy to focus on this.

The tournament we were in meant nothing. There were almost no college scouts at it. In fact, most of the college coaches had long ago offered their scholarships. Now they were looking for the few kids they could invite into school as walk-ons. There were no guarantees. Just a few kind words.

My conversation with Johnny Moser the day

after the awards assembly had been short and abrupt. I had apologized profusely for lying to him. I had told him I was very sorry for what I'd done.

"No problem," Moser had said. "But Duke's still withdrawing its scholarship offer. Good luck with your soccer career and your injury."

Then he'd hung up. See ya.

And just like that, my dreams of going to Duke and playing soccer there vanished.

If I had any hope of playing soccer in college, I would have to earn every minute of the time on the field—and pay for every dollar of the college's tuition. There would be no free ride. Those days were long, long gone. My father had been very clear about that. And although he'd never said he was disappointed about Duke, I knew he was.

I glanced around the field one more time to make sure. No college scouts. Only Mom and Joon, watching from the far sideline. Joon waved at me, encouraging me. I gave her a quick nod, then turned back to Asher.

"Go slow," Asher instructed. "Got it? Take it slow. Get the feel of the game. Let it come to you at first. See how you feel."

"Got it," I said, waving my arms around nervously.

I looked out at the squad that was starting to take the field. Once I would have ignored them, taken my spot on the field without a thought for who was on the other side opposite me. I'd never cared who was marking me. It had never mattered before.

degrees of betrayal

Now I sized up their marking backs. Could I handle them? How fast were they? Were they big? Were they physical?

"Ryun!" Asher said sharply. I jerked my focus back to him. "Those guys don't matter. They're just players. What matters is *you*—what you have inside of you, what you've learned the past seven months. Don't worry about them. Take care of yourself. Okay?"

I nodded, not sure I understood. But the game was about to start, and my time had run out.

The first ball they sent me was a long, through ball, out wide. I raced toward it at three-quarters speed. Their wing beat me to it, punched it out even wider around me, and cleared it back the other direction to their strikers. I wasn't even close.

I glanced over at Asher to see if he was worried. He wasn't even paying attention to me. He was following the ball at the other end of the field.

The next ball that came my way was a 50-50 ball. I got to it the same time their defensive midfielder did. I hesitated just as I got there. He didn't. He drove his leg right through the ball and me. He swept past me, cleaned up the loose ball, and raced away.

Finally, on about the sixth try, I got a ball free and clear in space. I took one touch, sent it out wide, and raced after it. I pushed the ball twice more with the outside of my right foot, running almost at top speed along with it.

Their marking back closed on me. I needed to make a move. I waited a fraction of a second too long, and he came sliding in at me, cleats low to the ground. He caught the ball first, then me. I went flying. The ball slid forward. The ref kept his hands in his pocket. It had been a clean slide tackle.

Every chance was like that. The first half ended in a scoreless tie. I had blown most of the chances that had come my way or simply let them fizzle. My teammates were sympathetic, but I could see that their patience was starting to wear thin. I needed to show them something. Or else they would quit on me. No question.

"So this is how it ends? Like this? Without even trying?" Asher asked me after his very brief half-time speech to the rest of the team.

"I'm doing my best," I said, afraid to look him in the eye.

"No," he said forcefully. "You're quitting on me. Which is something I never thought I'd see. Not from you." He walked away.

I wanted to follow him, tell him that it wasn't that way. But I knew—as Asher knew—that there was only one way to prove I wasn't going to quit. Sometimes words weren't enough. Sometimes only actions mattered, deeds on the field of battle.

I took my position on the right wing at the start of the second half. The handful of spectators, even the opposing players faded from view. I didn't care who was there anymore—coaches, Asher, Joon, my mom. There was only me and the ball. I had to know. I had to find out, once and for all.

Ten minutes into the second half, I got my chance. One of our center midfielders played the ball to my feet, out wide. I pivoted to my left, taking the defender with me toward the box.

I had to make a move. Right now. I planted my leg—the one hurt in the accident—and pushed off hard in the opposite direction. I went one way. The defender went another. The ball stayed at my feet. My leg didn't buckle.

A final defender closed on me deep inside the box. I had to make one more move, without fear. He started his slide tackle early, right at my legs. I didn't hesitate this time. I planted my leg again and popped the ball up with my foot at the same time. My leg—and the ball—cleared the slide tackle cleanly. I landed on the other side of him.

I hit the ground upright and, without thinking, fired a shot off with my bad leg without even breaking stride. The ball hit my laces perfectly, with the counterspin I wanted. It rocketed in with such force that the goalkeeper was still diving and hadn't landed by the time the ball hit the side netting for a goal.

Once I would have sprinted to the corner flag, pulled my jersey over my head, and taunted my opponents with my brilliance and talent. I would have yelled to the heavens and raised my hands in jubilation. I would have raced around the field, proclaiming my superiority.

But not today. And maybe never again.

Today I just slid to my knees and lowered my head, a few feet from the goal. I waited in silence, a kind of peace settling on me. The same kind of peace I'd felt that had given me the courage to tell my father the truth.

For all anyone knew, I was praying. And maybe I was, in the only way I knew how.

My teammates reached me an instant later and surrounded me. They piled on top of me, happy to have me back.

As I jogged toward the center of the field after my teammates had let me up, I looked over at Joon. She was trying to hide it from me, but I could see she was crying. Girls. I would never figure them out no matter how hard I tried. But I was sure glad that she was here to share this with me. She, of all people, deserved it.

As I took my place at the center, Asher moved over to within a few feet of me. "All luck," he said, trying his best not to smile. "Do it again and I'll believe."

"I will," I answered, free at last. "Just watch."

degrees OF betrayal

Betrayal comes naturally—
where you stand will determine who's
to blame—but there's always
more than one side to the story.

sierra's story
{DANDI DALEY MACKALL}

ryun's story
{JEFF NESBIT}

kenzie's story
{MELODY CARLSON}

For more inside info,
go to Degreesofbetrayal.com
and enter code betrayal02.

A Sneak Peek at *Sierra's Story* . . .

I'm trying so hard to remember that my head is splitting into pieces. I see white specks in the black, like tiny bone fragments. Who was with me? Not Ryun. *Please, God, not Ryun.*

But I can see myself behind the giant wheel of the old Chevy. I'm driving—to a football game. The last one of the season. I pick up Kenzie. And I know I'm driving to Ryun's.

Somebody tell me! Where are they? Are they okay? If I hurt them, I don't want to live. Is that why the police are here? I hurt McKenzie and Ryun? Did I kill them? Did I?

The room feels empty now. I want to scream for the police to come back so I can confess. *Yes! I did it! I don't remember, but I must have done this.* They won't believe me if I tell them I can't remember anything.

Not that I care if they believe me or not. It doesn't matter.

If I can ever talk again, I'll cry out so loud the whole state will hear me: "Yes! I did it. Bring on the judge. Bring on the gas pellets or the lethal needle. Take your pick. I don't care. Just let it be over."

Life, I mean. It might as well be.

■　　■　　■

"Hi, guys," I say, hoping I'm smiling warmly at both of them. Ryun's cheeks are red from the cold outside or the warmth of the hospital.

"We wanted to see how you're doing," Ryun says, not looking at me.

"Take off your coats," I urge.

"We can't stay," Kenzie says.

Ryun nods at her, then explains, "Yeah. I need to get to work."

Kenzie smiles. "You look good."

Ryun comes to my bed and kisses the top of my head. "Sorry we can't stay and talk and stuff." His gaze darts around the room.

Kenzie looks nervous.

They're making *me* nervous. Part of me wants them to leave. But that doesn't make sense. I hate it when they're not here. I'm so mixed-up. I feel like screaming.

Kenzie tugs Ryun's arm, as if to pull him toward the door.

The gesture jars me. Ice water shoots through my spine.

And just that fast, I know that I'm right. My best friend and my boyfriend. I'm on the wrong end of a country-western song.

"We should go," she says. And the *we* means something, something huge, something unfair.

Ryun looks at her the way he used to look at me—expectant, familiar. What they have isn't friendship. It's more than friendship. I can see that.

They leave, and I imagine them walking out of the hospital, their arms around each other. I picture them getting into Ryun's car. He opens the door. She slides in. He helps her fasten her seat belt. The engine starts. They're off on a romantic sunset drive together.

Or maybe not. Maybe they're going out for burgers at Riley's. I speed up the image, making them go faster and faster, pressing Ryun's foot to the floor. Kenzie reaches for his arm again, just like she did in my hospital room. Only now I imagine Ryun, jerking his hand away, shocked at Kenzie's move. The car drifts off the road. He pulls it back, but it's too sharp. The car flips over.

And *bang!* Missouri and I have two new room-mates.

That part about the car flipping? I'm wondering if that's my subconscious trying to work its way up. Because the car I'm picturing isn't Ryun's car. It's the Chevy. Dad's '57 Chevy. And the sign in the background isn't Riley's. It's Route 58, where Officer McCarthy said the car went off the road. The scene of the accident.

A Sneak Peek at *Kenzie's Story* ...

I tried to act natural, but I was in total shock. I'd come down to the University of Virginia thinking this college visit would be pretty boring, but then someone (my guardian angel maybe) went and paired me off with none other than the guy of my dreams—Highview High's soccer king *Ryun Lee!*

Talk about unreal! Who would've thought something like this could happen to me? But there I was, staring into the face of the coolest guy on the planet—the guy I'd had a secret crush on for, well, like forever. I casually said, "Hey," as I joined him in the backseat of our escort's car, but I couldn't help thinking, *What is up with this? Have I died and gone to heaven?*

Just the same, I couldn't figure out why Ryun Lee would be wasting his time visiting a college like the

University of Virginia when everyone knew he was getting some incredible scholarship offers from the really big schools—like Duke.

I had to remind myself to play it cool. No way was I going to blow the new image I'd worked so hard to create over the last couple of months. You are a new woman, McKenzie Parker, I told myself. And your time has finally come!

"How's your game going this summer?" I asked as our escort, a Billy something or other, put the car into gear.

Ryun gave me a confused look. "It's going fine."

I nodded and leaned back, thankful that I'd decided to wear the sundress Sierra talked me into buying on our most recent shopping spree. It was a two-piece number with a halter top that fit like skin and an adorable little skirt that swirled nicely and showed off my tanned legs. Sierra assured me it was perfect for me and even said the color brought out the gold flecks in my brown eyes. She also insisted on picking out the coolest shoes I'd ever owned in my life—Nine Wests with high heels and skinny straps. Of course, because Sierra helped, they went perfectly with the sundress.

As I sat in the car, I felt like laughing. Ryun looked so dazed and confused, like he couldn't place who I was or how I knew him. It was obvious he had no idea who the strange chick sitting beside him really was. I felt sorry for him, so I finally gave him a break. "You don't remember me, do you?"

He made a funny face. "Well, I'm not sure. You seem familiar."

degrees of betrayal

I stretched out my hand. "McKenzie Parker."

He nodded and shook my hand, holding on a second or two longer than you'd normally do. And the feeling of him holding my hand like that and looking into my eyes made me feel warm and tingly all over. Almost dizzy.

"McKenzie Parker," he repeated, but it was obvious he was still clueless.

"Remember we worked on the yearbook together?"

His raised eyebrow showed he was even more surprised. *THAT McKenzie?* I could tell he was thinking. But since he's a gentleman, he didn't even mention my prior life as the invisible girl.

Still, it was fun watching him study me, as if seeing me for the first time. And I got this feeling that he liked what he saw too. Just the same, I was careful to keep my distance. I mean, as much as I liked Ryun and have always liked Ryun, I didn't want to move in on Sierra's turf. Everyone knew that she and Ryun had been a "thing" since the spring of junior year. And I knew enough about Sierra and her friends to know that it wouldn't be good for me if I did something sleazy like that. But it sure wasn't *my* fault we'd been stuck together for the evening. Besides, we were only doing a little tour of the campus and then heading over to a party at a frat house. Totally innocent.

After a few minutes, I couldn't help but bring up Sierra's name. For one thing, I was curious. If they were still dating, and I assumed they were since she hadn't told me otherwise, then why didn't he invite her to come along with him? Besides that, I wanted to see how he reacted. Because, although I certainly wasn't an expert on these matters, I thought Ryun Lee was actually *flirting* with me. He'd already complimented me on my new look several times. There was just something about those smoldering dark eyes that told me he liked the new me.

■   ■   ■

Before the night was over, I could feel myself falling—make that plummeting—in love with the guy I'd had a crush on for ages. The guy I talked to in my dreams and in my head every time he walked by.

We talked for several hours, but it seemed like minutes. I felt like Cinderella, knowing our time would end and we'd both turn back into ourselves and go back home to Highview. Then Sierra, the incredibly cool and popular Sierra, would have her guy back by her side again and I'd just be on the fringes, where I usually was. Still, Why not make the best of tonight? I asked myself. Really make it a night to remember?

Jeff Nesbit has written 16 inspirational novels for children, teens, and adults. He has been a national journalist and worked in senior positions in the U.S. Senate, the Food and Drug Administration, and the White House. His young adult bestsellers include the High Sierra Adventure series. Several of his books have been translated and sold around the world.

Jeff, his wife, Casey, and their children live in Waterford, Virginia, where they raise horses. All three of his children—Josh, Elizabeth, and Daniel—are avid soccer players. Jeff runs a very successful consulting practice, including creating major projects for the Discovery Channel and Yale University. You can find out more about his career at www.shilohcommunications.com

areUthirsty.com
Degreesofbetrayal.com

degrees OF guilt

Sammy's dead...they each played a part.
Kyra, his twin sister. Miranda, the girl he
loved. And Tyrone, a friend from school.

WHAT'S THE REAL STORY?

There's always more than
one point of view—read all three.

kyra's story
{DANDI DALEY MACKALL}
ISBN 0-8423-8284-4

miranda's story
{MELODY CARLSON}
ISBN 0-8423-8283-6

tyrone's story
{SIGMUND BROUWER}
ISBN 0-8423-8285-2

degreesofguilt.com

Are you a *Lord of the Rings* junkie?

WANT MORE?

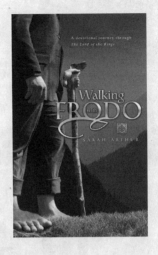

Check out *Walking with Frodo*...a devotional that uses Tolkien's stories to lead you through nine pairs of choices – darkness or light, betrayal or loyalty, deception or honesty, to name just a few – and reveals what the Bible has to say about each.

aRe you Ready foR The challenge?

areUthirsty.com

ISBN 0-8423-8554-1

New from Sarah Arthur

COMING 2005

WALKING WITH

Bilbo

continue the journey. . .

If you ever need a shoulder to cry on or a hand to hold, mine can reach all the way across the world.

best friends . . .
an ocean apart . . .
surviving life together

Hands across the
MOON

jane g. meyer

★ Life isn't what best friends Gretchen and Mia had in mind. They'd looked forward to their junior year together—in California. Then Gretchen had to move to Ecuador . . . a world away. Now, nothing's going right for either of them.

Sometimes it seems that their "across the moon" letters are their best lifeline.

areUthirsty.com
ISBN 0-8423-8286-0